RAVISH

Marie Tuhart

RAVISH

He wants nothing more than to ravish her for the rest of their lives.

Easygoing leather store owner and whip-maker Colby Durham embraces whatever life throws at him. Now, he wants café owner Lara Meyer bound to him in every way possible. When Lara's hired to cater an event at Wicked Sanctuary, Colby finally gets his chance. He's tired of being alone and has wanted to start a relationship with Lara for a while. But will she understand the need for kink in his life?

Lara's world has been filled with wealth and status, not that she cares. She broke away from her controlling family years ago and defied them again when she opened her café. When Colby enters her life, Lara finds herself entranced by this unusual man. He dresses leather, owns a leather shop, and knows and occasionally rides with bikers. But as much as she might want to get into a relationship with Colby, her family won't leave her business and love life alone. If they discover what's going on between her and Colby, it could ruin her chance at future happiness.

Together, Lara and Colby must negotiate a bond that can stand the test of outside forces.

ACKNOWLEGMENTS

There are several people I want to thank for supporting me through this book:

Laurie, thank you for reading the book more than once and all the brainstorming help.

Nia, Isabel, and Susannah, thank you for all our sprinting sessions.

Red Quill Editing team, you are the best team to work with.

Publisher's Note: This book contains a dominant male, spunky heroine, sexy situations, and food.

To My Readers:

This book contains elements of the BDSM lifestyle that are only true to life in this book. There are various relationship dynamics in the lifestyle, which are decided between the people involved. While I have researched and talked with people in the lifestyle, this is my take on how my characters choose to live.

If you decide to explore the lifestyle yourself, please remember to always be safe. Never go home with someone you don't know. Attend a munch or a small get-together first to see if this is something you want in your life. Reading and living are very different.

There is no mention of the coronavirus that exists in our world right now. I purposely left it out. This is a place for you to escape.

Enjoy.

Chapter 1

Lara Meyer rolled her eyes as she made her way out from behind the counter of her café, Sweet and Savory. Her brother Keith, and Walter, her ex-husband, stood near the bikers who were having lunch.

"Keith, Walter, stop bothering my customers and leave."

Both men turned to her. "They're nothing but scum and thieves," her brother said.

The bikers stiffened.

"Oh, grow up." She got between her brother, her ex, and the bikers.

"These men," her brother sneered, "will get you closed down faster than rats."

"The only rats I see are the two standing in front of me." Damn, she had no idea why Keith and the ex seemed to hate the bikers.

"We're not the ones making trouble," Walter said, putting a hand on her shoulder.

She stiffened, trying to tamp down the instant fear that swept over her. *It's okay.* She reminded herself. He couldn't do anything here. Lara stepped away so Walter's hand fell away. One of the bikers stood up, and Lara feared there would be a fight.

"Enough." Lara pushed her brother and ex in their chests, making them fall back two steps. She turned her head. "I'm okay, Monty," she told the biker. He was a big guy.

"Fine, but if you need us, yell." He sat back down.

The door to the café opened, and Lara almost let out a groan. Colby Durham, owner of Durham's Leather shop, strode in. His raven hair was mussed and his green eyes assessing. The bikers frequented his shop and, most of the time, would come to her café for food. She hadn't been sure of the group or Colby's shop in the beginning, but the past few months had improved her business, and there'd never been a lick of trouble until now.

Not that Lara minded the increase in business, but every time she saw Colby, her heart sped up a little. She didn't have time for men, especially ones who made her think of all the naughty things they could do to her.

"Problem?" Colby asked as he strode over to her.

"Nothing that I can't handle," Lara huffed. She didn't want him involved. Her brothers and ex were always in here making comments, but this was the first time they did it around a table full of bikers. The last thing she wanted was a fight to break out.

Colby nodded and took a seat with the bikers.

"Time for you two to leave," Lara said.

"Not until they do," Keith said.

Lara swore silently. "They are having lunch while you two are doing nothing but making a scene." She fought her temper down; it wouldn't do to lose it in front of all her customers.

The door opened again. Who'd called the police? She looked over at the counter where her employee, Eve, nodded. At least one of them was thinking straight.

"See, the police are here to arrest the riff-raff," Keith said.

"The only riff-raff is you," Lara shot back.

"Officer Logan Wolfe, what seems to be the problem?"

"The problem is those bikers," Walter said, waving his hand at them.

"Officer Wolfe, the bikers are not the problem. These two are." She pointed at her brother and her ex. "They've come into my café making accusations about customers who are just minding their own business, and they won't leave."

"I see." The officer looked over Keith and Walter. "Gentlemen, if you'd please come outside with me."

"Do you know who I am?" Keith puffed out his chest.

"Actually, I do, Mr. Meyer."

Colby stood up and looked at the officer. "Officer Wolfe, if you need a witness, the two men here were harassing the bikers when I came in." Colby's voice was calm, and Lara found herself relaxing for the first time since her brother and ex walked in.

"Of course there's a problem, and you're part of it," Keith said. "Your leather shop is bringing in a criminal element."

"Oh for goodness sake, Keith. These men are not criminals and neither is Colby."

"I don't think you realize," Keith went on, ignoring her completely, "I can ruin you all."

Lara's temper flared. She hated it when her family flaunted their wealth. That was one of the reasons she had very little to do with them. "You might, but do you have enough money for all the lawsuits that will be coming your way? Especially the one from me?"

"All right," Officer Wolfe said. "That's enough. Outside Mr. Meyer, and you too." Office Wolfe pointed at Walter. "Now," his tone hard.

Keith glared at her. "Very well." He turned and

marched to toward the door.

"This isn't over," Walter muttered as he followed.

Lara clasped her hands together so no one would see them shaking. She turned to the bikers.

"I'm sorry, guys."

"Not your fault," the biker who stood to defend her earlier said.

"Please stay as long as you want, and I'll have Eve refill your beverages," Lara turned, and Colby was right there.

"Are you okay?" he asked, his green eyes filled with concern.

"I'm fine. Just angry." Angry and scared. Confrontation wasn't her strong suit, but she wasn't about to let anyone harass her customers. She marched away and went behind the counter. She saw Colby grab an empty chair and sit down to talk to the bikers. "Eve, please refill their drinks, and see if Mr. Durham wants anything. On the house."

"Sure thing." Eve sauntered out from behind the counter.

Lara kept a smile on her face as customers began to show up and order. At least this had happened before the lunchtime rush, or the entire town would have seen what happened. She almost laughed, since she was sure it was already making news on the gossip tree.

She glanced out the front window of the café to see Officer Wolfe talking with Keith and Walter. Yep, she was pretty sure her Aunt Tammy would hear all about this before long.

Lara kept smiling for customer after customer. Officer Logan walked back in and talked with Colby and the bikers, then came to the counter. She explained her side of the story, and he told her not to hesitate to call if she needed help.

A little while later, she saw the bikers had left. Colby had switched to a smaller table as Eve hustled over to the now empty table to wipe it off. It was hardly necessary. Those guys always cleaned up after themselves.

It was after one when the lunch rush started to subside, and Lara could draw a deep breath. She thought she'd be used to it, but today seemed busier than normal. Maybe it was time to get more help in here. Well, she did have Megan, her other employee. Time to see if they could work out a better schedule.

"I'm going to do refills on coffee," Lara told Eve as she picked up the two carafes, one regular, one decaf, and made her way around the café, refilling cups as needed. She paused at the table where Colby sat by the window.

"More coffee?" she asked.

"Yes, please. Regular." His deep voice sent a frisson of delight over her skin.

She poured his coffee and was about to turn away when he spoke again.

"Thank you for protecting my friends." He paused. "Who were the two idiots?"

"My brother and my ex, and you don't have to thank me. The bikers are good guys."

"I'm a good guy too." He grinned at her.

"Jury is still out on that." She walked away, but a smile teased her lips. While Colby might raise her blood pressure in a good way, she didn't need a man in her life.

The café door opened, and Sierra and Max breezed through the doorway. "Lara," Sierra called out, making a beeline for the counter. Max saw Colby, walked over, and sat down.

Sierra and her friends Crystal and Tessa came to the café all the time. Heck, Crystal stopped by here most mornings for coffee and breakfast.

"Hi, Sierra. What can I do you for you today?"

"Do you have a minute to chat?"

"Sure." The lunch rush was gone, so she had a little time. "Eve, I'll be right back." Lara slipped out from behind the counter and led Sierra over to an empty table. She glanced over at Max and Colby. A rush of heat filled her veins. Two different, yet alike men. They both had that...dominant—the only word that fit—air to them.

"What did you want to talk about?" Lara asked, turning her attention back to Sierra.

"I was wondering if you'd be willing to cater an event at the club?"

Lara stared at Sierra. She knew, as did most of the town, about Wicked Sanctuary. After the press conference two weeks ago, involving Tessa and Damon, it was all people were talking about.

"It depends on what level of catering you're looking for." Most of her food was for quick lunches and snacks.

"Nothing big. Mainly appetizers and desserts."

Lara pulled her phone out of her pocket and brought up the note pad. "That's doable. Do you know what you're looking for?"

"Your mac and cheese bites for sure and at least two or three more appetizers. For desserts, how about brownies, cookies, and those lovely mini cupcakes."

She made notes. "Would you like some fruit cups for those who don't want sweets?"

"Oh yes, that would be nice."

"How many people?"

Sierra frowned. "I'd have to ask Max for an exact

count, but I would say at least fifty, maybe seventy-five."

"Okay. I use gel chafing fuel to keep the food warm."

"We have a strict fire code at the club."

"I understand. I'll make sure it's safe." She ran items through her head. Big metal pans to hold the food, holders, fuel, tongs, plates, napkins. "Are there electrical outlets near where you want the tables, or will I need to run extension cords?"

"I think so." Sierra let out a sigh. "I've never really looked."

"I'll make a note to ask Max. I have a couple of hot boxes that I can keep extra food warm in. This way we don't have to worry about anything going bad."

"Makes sense."

"When is this party?"

Sierra dipped her head. "Ummm, Saturday."

"It's a good thing today is Monday." It gave her time to order what she needed and Saturday to get it all ready.

"Sorry. Max decided on the small party just yesterday."

"No worries. I've worked with less time." Lara smiled. She'd been curious about the club for a while now, so at least she'd get to see the inside of it. Lara glanced over at Max and Colby. She wondered if Colby played?

What was she thinking? She was aware of the lifestyle and even dabbled a bit when she was in college, but since coming home... She'd been to a munch or two, but nothing else. When the club opened, she'd just married Walter. "Bad mistake," she muttered.

"Sorry, I missed that," Sierra said.

Lara shook her head. "I was thinking out loud. Once I get a firm number of people, I can do some number crunching for you and let you know about the costs. Then I can get a standard contract drawn up for Max to sign."

"That sounds good."

"What sounds good?" Max asked, striding up to the table.

Lara watched Colby open the door to leave, but at the last second, he looked back. Their gazes met, and he winked. Lara lowered her eyes as her face grew warm.

"Lara agreed to do the party. She'll get a cost for us, and if we agree, a contract."

"Perfect. Thank you, Lara."

"Not a problem. Who were you using for catering before now?" Lara did a little here and there, but she always liked to hear who her competition was, so to speak.

Max pulled out a chair and sat down. "Usually we don't cater our parties. We might have some fruit and veggies, but that's about it."

"Then why now?" Lara was curious.

"We wanted to try something new. A members only party with food. I do have some pretty strict rules about where the food can be."

"Understandable." Lara started running the menu through her head.

"Also I'll need you to sigh an NDA for the club," Max said.

"Oh?" That was a surprise.

"Yes, as I said, strict rules," Max smiled.

"Can you email it to me?" Lara asked.

"Will do. Anything else you need to know?" he asked.

They talked for another ten minutes. Lara got the information she needed about the electrical outlets and the number of people. She gave him a rough idea of the cost. Max told her to just email him the contract; the price wasn't an issue. He also advised her to arrive a little early on Saturday so he could show her the area where he wanted the food.

After they left, Lara began cleaning off tables and wiping them down. Eve left at two-thirty, and Lara was putting things away when Colby walked back in.

"Good, I caught you before you closed for the day," he said, striding up to the counter.

"What can I do for you?" She almost rolled her eyes at her own question.

"I wanted to know if you've had any trouble with the bikers?"

Lara tilted her head. "No, they're all really good customers. Never a problem. Is this about this morning?"

"A little. I was worried, not so much about the guys from this morning, but that other bikers might be causing you trouble, and if so, I'd talk with them."

"No, they're fine. The trouble makers were my brother and my ex."

"Ex?" His eyebrows rose.

"Ex-husband. Four years now, thank goodness."

"Sounds like there's a story there."

"A long and boring one."

"You could never tell a boring story." He leaned against the counter. "I'm glad the guys aren't causing you any issues. They really enjoy your food."

"They do?" Lara stared at Colby. The bikers came in and ordered the same things most days.

"Do you know how many places carry gluten-free or wheat-free food?"

Lara paused. "Doesn't everyone?"

Colby laughed and a tingle of awareness invaded her veins. "No. Plus you have sugar free desserts and fruit thingies."

"Fruit thingies?" A giggle escaped her lips.

"You know those little cup things that look like miniature waffle cones."

"Oh, the tart shells."

"Not to mention, you also have vegetarian options."

"I never realized." She'd added those items to the menu when people started asking for them.

"So, if you ever have any problems with them, come get me, or better yet, call me." He turned her order pad around and wrote his number. "I mean it. If you ever need me, give me a call. That's my cell."

Her belly clenched. Oh, did he do midnight booty calls? Lara closed her eyes. How would it feel to have his hands skim over her belly as she buried her fingers in his black hair? Okay, she'd been reading way too many erotic romance novels lately. Her mind was running away with her body's needs.

"I will. If I need you." Was that her breathless voice?

"Good. Be safe. See you Saturday night." He sauntered out of the café.

Lara locked the door, flipped the neon sign off, and paused. Did he say he'd see her Saturday night? He did. Her heart fluttered. Now she really had a reason to look forward to Saturday night.

Chapter 2

Saturday night, Lara stared at the back of her small SUV. It was stacked full. She had two hot boxes there, and the back seat held napkins, plates, tongs, and two coolers keeping the spiral wraps cold.

She'd had both Eve and Megan in the café today while she prepared everything for tonight. Excitement filled her body. Not only to see Wicked Sanctuary, but also because she'd see Colby again.

He'd stayed away from the café all week. One of the regular bikers, Monty, let it slip he was ordering stuff for Colby and taking it back to his shop.

Lara wondered about that but figured maybe Colby was busy. He did have a shop to run, and she had no reason to feel hurt at not seeing him until tonight. Now her nerves tingled with the idea of seeing him at the club. Max had commented it was a party for members only, so Colby had to be a member.

Pulling up the directions Max had given her, Lara pulled out of her parking spot and began the drive. The club was on the outskirts of Pleasant Valley. She'd given herself plenty of time to get there and set up. Max told her he'd make sure the tables were all ready for her.

Her favorite song came on the radio, and she moved her head and shoulders to the beat as she drove, thinking about her week. At least her brother and ex hadn't been back to the café. That was a good thing.

But her mother had called her several times, asking her why she called the police on them. Lara told her she hadn't called, but they needed to learn to listen when she told them to leave. She had a business to run.

Her aunt Tammy had rolled her eyes and muttered about how her nephews were too much like their father. At times, Lara agreed with her. Her brothers both worked at the bank her father owned. Hell, even her ex worked there.

Lara's fingers tightened around the steering wheel. Her father had wanted her to get a degree in finance. So dry and boring. There was no way she was going to go for that. He finally compromised when she was accepted to Berkeley. He called Berkeley a hippy-dippy school, but as long as she went to the Haas Business School, he'd allow it.

Best decision she ever made. She might be a bit lousy with numbers, but she'd learned a lot about being an entrepreneur by visiting the cafés around the university. Small ones, large ones, chains, mom and pop places. She'd go to different ones every day, scope out what they were serving, how they treated their customers, especially students. It gave her ideas, and her final paper had been on the service industry.

Lara spied her turnoff and slowed down. She stopped at the big metal gate. Rolling down her window, she rang the button on the call box.

"How can I help you?" a deep male voice asked.

"Hi, I'm Lara, the caterer for tonight."

"Yes. The gate will open in a moment, please drive through. Park close to the door."

"Thank you." The ornate gates began to open, and Lara drove through. She loved how the trees lined the driveway, then the view widened. Lara almost stopped her vehicle.

"It's beautiful." The club was bigger than she thought. She hadn't expected it to look like a well-maintained mansion, but dingier, like an underground club or something. Any last nervousness she had around the club disappeared. She pulled up and parked near the front door as instructed, then hopped out. Before she could make it to the back of her vehicle, Colby and Max walked out.

Her heart sped up. Colby was wearing black pants and a black t-shirt with heavy boots. Damn, that man filled out his clothing. What would he look like out of them? Shaking her lusty thoughts away, she opened the back.

"How the heck did you get those into your SUV?" Colby asked, looking at the hot boxes.

"I had some help." Eve's boyfriend and his friend had come over and helped her load them into her SUV.

Colby stared at her. "You could have called me."

Lara opened her mouth, but Max spoke up.

"Why don't we get these out," Max said, giving her a wink.

"Please. Let me get the rolling cart to put them on." Lara opened the passenger door, pulled out the cart, and unfolded it. Colby watched her with a frown.

"Perfect," Max said.

Lara stood back and watched the muscles bunch in Colby's arms and shoulders as he unloaded the food. Did he work out? *Get your mind back on business.* Once the two hot boxes were on the cart, she followed Max and Colby inside.

"Ralph, this is Lara."

"Miss Lara."

"Hi, Ralph." He sat behind a desk, which she assumed was to check people into the club. She followed the men through the first doorway and then through the second one.

Inside the second door, she stopped. So, this was a BDSM club. She looked around as she followed the two men.

She saw various areas set up with equipment. Spanking benches, massage tables, and some other equipment she didn't recognize. There was a bar—she'd have to ask Max about that. Sofas and overstuffed chairs sat around the room, and one area was painted green. The lighting was subtle, but there was enough illumination to move around safely. Against the back wall, where they were headed, four long tables were set up with white tablecloths.

"Where do you want these?" Max asked.

"On the floor is fine, but close to the outlet. I'm trusting I won't have an issue if I plug both in?"

"Not unless you pull a hell of a lot of voltage, which I don't think will happen."

"Nope." As they placed them on the floor, Lara knelt down and plugged them in. "Thank you for setting up the tables. I'll go get the rest of my stuff and get everything set up."

"We'll help," Colby said.

"I don't want to hold you up if you have other things to do."

She felt the intensity of Colby's stare, and her skin prickled. "Okay, let's do it."

With three of them, it only took two more trips to her car to empty it.

"What else can we do to help?" Max asked.

"Not much really, I'll get the stands up." She pulled out the metal stands and set them on the tables, then pulled out the cans of gel to keep the food warm in the pans. Lara pulled out the lighter.

"Let me do that," Colby said, covering her hand with his.

Lara shrugged and gave Colby the lighter. "Only light the ones for the first rack." She'd light the others ones as time got closer, but she wanted to have some items out for early birds. She saw Max staring at the gel chafing fuel cans. "Is there going to be a problem?" she asked Max. They'd talked about it.

"No. I've got two fire extinguishers here by the tables." He pointed them out to her. "Plus others behind the bar and in other places."

"Good." She noted where the extinguishers were. "I do have a question." She looked at Max.

"Yes."

"You have a bar, so I take it you serve alcohol?"

Max grinned. "We do not."

Lara blinked. "You don't?" Interesting.

"No, we provide water, juice, and soda. The only time we have alcohol is when I do a special party, and there is no play that night."

Lara liked that. "Good. I was wondering if I'd have to watch for drunk patrons."

"You shouldn't unless they're drunk before the get here, and we watch carefully." Max lifted his hand. "If you have any issues, let me know or Colby. It will be taken care of."

"Yes, it will be dealt with." Colby held the lighter out to her. She took it and put it away. Napkins, plates, and utensils made it to the table, along with tongs. Satisfied, Lara knelt and pulled two trays out. She placed them in the holder and lifted the lids.

"Oh my God," Sierra said, rushing across the room. "Mac and cheese bites." Grabbing a napkin, she took one out of the pan.

Max glared at Sierra, and Lara laughed. "I put these out

for all of you. Please, have some."

"From Sierra, I know one is mac and cheese bites, but what is the other?" Colby asked.

"Spinach, artichoke, and rice."

Using the tongs she'd set out, Colby lifted one out and put it on a napkin before picking it up and raising it to his mouth.

Lara watched those sensuous lips open and white teeth bite into the food. How would those lips feel against her skin? Would he nip with his teeth or just kiss and lick her skin. Heat filled her body.

"Nice and crunchy. Really good flavor," Colby said.

"I'll have to try those next," Sierra announced, reaching for the one Max had on his napkin.

"Get your own." Max gently slapped the back of her hand.

Sierra stuck her lower lip out and picked up one for herself.

Lara grinned at the way Max and Sierra teased each other. The love flowed from them. She turned away. Had she ever been in love like that? Maybe at first with Walter, but she couldn't be sure.

She'd met her ex at Berkeley and fallen in love – at least it felt that way. And when he followed her back to Pleasant Valley, she thought it was destiny. More like a horror story with and ending that still plagued her.

Colby's voice snapped her out of her momentary flashback.

"What else did you bring?" Colby asked.

"I made some pinwheel sandwiches, deep dish pizza bites, bagel dogs, and roasted veggie tart. And of course, desserts."

"You're going to spoil everyone," Colby said.

"I hope so." This might be something she could incorporate into her business. Catering small events for appetizers and desserts.

"Sounds like you thought of everything."

"I tried. Sierra wasn't sure, so I wanted to make sure I had some vegetarian stuff, gluten-free, and regular menu items."

"What is that smell?" Tessa walked into the club along with Damon.

"Hey, Tessa," Lara said.

"Sierra got you to cater. Oh goodness, what did you bring?" Tessa all but ran to the table and grabbed a napkin.

Lara couldn't help but laugh. While the three women had been in her café often, they tended to eat the same things. Actually, most of her customers did. She needed to expand their horizons.

"Hi, Lara," Damon said, coming up behind Tessa.

"Damon."

"Are you ready for tonight?" Damon asked Colby.

"Yes. Oh, that reminds me. I have the wristbands for you to try out. Be right back."

Lara watched Colby stride across the room. Oh that man had one hell of a tight backside in those pants. That's when she noticed that the men all seemed to be dressed alike, but where Colby had boots on, the others had on loafers.

Sierra and Tessa had on corsets and short skirts with ballet type shoes. Lara looked down at her pants and shirt. She was going to stick out like a sore thumb.

"You're fine," Sierra whispered.

"But..."

"Sierra's right," Max spoke. "As the caterer, what you're wearing is fine. Tonight, you're here as a guest. So feel free to walk around the club." When Colby came back, he was holding a bunch of silicone bracelets. Max plucked a white one out of Colby's hand. "Your wrist please."

Lara held out her left wrist. Max fastened the bracelet. "What is this for?"

"We have a color coded system for Doms and subs," Colby said. "The one you're wearing signifies that you're new and not ready to play yet."

"Oh." Lara's cheeks grew warm. She watched as Max put a purple and white one on Sierra. Damon put a pink and white one on Tessa. Max and Damon took black, where Colby took blue.

She glanced up at Colby. "What do the colors purple and white, pink and white, black and blue mean?" She was curious about the other colors.

"Mine is a taken sub," Sierra said. "Tessa's is taken sub with medium experience."

"Max and Damon are black for being Masters in the club. And Colby blue for being a Dom," Tessa said.

"These turned out really nice, Colby." Max raised his wrist, looking at the silicone.

"I'll let you decide who you want to give them to. Once we get some feedback, I'll make as many as you need. I'm assuming, like the others, members will keep their wristbands," Colby said.

"Yes. That means, Lara, you can keep yours even if you don't join us after tonight," Max said.

"Oh. I'd love to join, but I don't think I can afford it."

Five jaws dropped open.

"What did I say?"

"You're into the lifestyle?" Tessa recovered first.

"Kind of blurted that out, didn't I?" Lara ducked her head. How could she have done that? Maybe because she felt comfortable around them. More so than her own family, except her aunt.

Warm fingers cupped her chin. "Nothing to be ashamed of." Colby's soft voice caressed her cheek.

Lara raised her gaze to meet his and found his green eyes alight with promise. She inhaled, trying to control the urge to fall into his arms.

As if Colby knew what she was thinking, his lips turned up. "I'm glad you're interested." He took her left hand in his.

A flutter of excitement flowed through her body.

"Why don't we make sure the equipment is ready?" Max said.

"Yes, we should," Damon commented.

Colby's grin widened. "Until later." He raised her hand to his lips and kissed her knuckles before lowering it and moving away with the men.

"Oh my goodness," Tessa said, fanning herself.

"Lara, I think you just found yourself a partner," Sierra said.

The flutter became a flock of butterflies in her belly. Maybe she had. The two women wandered off, and Lara glanced at her watch. Seven forty-five. Max told her the club opened at eight, so she'd better get the rest of the food out.

* * * *

For the next two hours, Lara stayed by the food tables, not only making sure there was enough food, but to answer any questions. Several people were happy she had some gluten-free pinwheel sandwiches and other vegetarian options.

The food was going over well. That made her happy. A man walked up to her, and she automatically looked at his wrist. She'd been doing that all night. Blue. Dom. He stood, looking over the food.

"Do you have a question?"

His blond hair curled at the ends, and his blue eyes twinkled. "The food is all very good."

"Thank you."

"I see that you're new. Would you like to walk around with me?" He smiled. "I'm Bennett, by the way."

"Max gave me this bracelet because I'm here as his guest to do the food." Bennett's smile started to fade. "But I'd love to walk around with you. I'm curious. Let me just make sure everything is good here." Lara checked the pans. "I'm ready."

"All right. How much do you know about the lifestyle?"

* * * *

Colby kept an eye on Lara. Everyone who'd come up to the food table would speak with her for a minute or so, then pick out their food and wander away. Having the food was a big hit for the club tonight.

When Bennett approached, Colby frowned. His conversation with Lara was animated, then Bennett took Lara by the elbow and led her away from the food.

Colby almost intervened, but stopped himself. Max had told Lara she could wander around the club, and she had the right to tour the club with whomever she wanted, but he wanted it to be him. Colby made his way to the scene Bennett and Lara had stopped to observe.

A simple spanking scene. Colby stayed off to the side. Lara's face was flushed as she watched the scene. Aroused maybe? She didn't look scared or uncomfortable in any way. When Bennett tried to put his arm around her shoulder, Lara shrugged it off and said something.

Bennett laughed and replied. Lara laughed too. Interesting exchange. When the spanking scene ended, they moved to a bondage scene. This time, Bennett didn't try to touch Lara. Good.

Colby's Dom instincts were running on high. Lara was his. But she hadn't told him that yet. He couldn't go all Neanderthal on her or Bennett—even if he wanted to.

"Keeping an eye on her?" Max asked, coming up beside Colby.

"Yeah." He wouldn't lie.

"Good. Bennett is a good Dom, but a little too new yet."

"Lara is new too."

"Something tells me that Lara has a bit of experience under her belt. She's taken in the members of the club rather well." Max waved his hand.

Colby was about to ask what he meant when one of the subs walked by him, nude. "Ah yes." Max was right. Outside of a couple times Lara froze up, she'd taken the different modes of dress or undress in stride.

"You're off shift soon. Make sure you claim her." Max walked away.

Colby shook his head. Would he ever understand how Max seemed to know everything? Another Dom called his name, and Colby went to see what he needed.

At midnight, Colby sighed. His shift was over. He made his way over to the food tables where Lara was checking on the various dishes.

He grabbed a bagel dog and ate it. Usually, he wasn't hungry, but smelling the food all night had his stomach growling.

"Hi, Colby," Lara said, straightening from the boxes that held the food.

"Hi. Are you getting ready to leave?" He'd hoped she would walk around the club with him.

"Not just yet." She shifted from one foot to the other.

Was she nervous? She hadn't seemed to be with Bennett earlier. He picked up a plate and began filling it. "Have you eaten?"

"A little."

"Will you fill a plate and come sit with me?" He kept his tone light; he didn't want to make her any more nervous than she already was.

"I'd like that." She smiled and picked up a plate. When she was ready, Colby led her over to a relatively quiet area in a corner of the club. He pulled two chairs close.

"Do you want something to drink?" he asked as he set his plate on his chair.

"Water, please."

"Be right back." Colby maneuvered his way over to the bar, retrieved two bottles of water, and returned to Lara. She was gazing around the club. The crowd had thinned out some.

He leaned over and set the water bottles on the floor between them before he picked up his plate and sat down. "You know, you surprised everyone earlier with the comment that you'd like to join the club."

Lara's hand waved in the air. "I didn't mean to. But I do have to admit everyone's expressions were a bit comical."

"Are you seriously interested?" Colby fought against the excitement pressing against his skin.

"I wouldn't have said that if I wasn't. But I don't know how I can afford it."

"It's more reasonable than you think." Colby paused. "If you want to see if you'd like it, you can come as my guest."

Her eyes widened. She hadn't expected that. Good. He wanted nothing more than to play with her in the club.

"You'd let me play with another Dom?"

Colby sat his empty plate down and crossed his arms over his chest. "No." He'd be honest with her. "I want to play with you. So, if you come as my guest, you only play with me. But I can't stop you if you join."

Lara's hand fluttered to her throat. "How do we know if we're compatible?"

His muscles relaxed. At least she was thinking about it and not shooting him down. "There's a questionnaire we can go through together." His gaze captured hers. "I believe in honesty, so here goes. I've watched you, Lara. The way you move, the way you talk to your customers, even tonight. I'm very attracted to you, and I believe we'd be good together."

She swallowed. "I do too." Lara leaned over and sat her plate on the floor. "Why did you have someone pick up food for you this week?"

Colby was surprised by the question. "Because I didn't want to jump the gun, so to speak, for tonight." He paused, gathering his thoughts. "I'd hoped you'd want to play."

Lara took a long drink of her water before setting it back down. "I have some experience in the lifestyle."

"Explain *some* to me, please." He exhaled. She wasn't shutting him down.

"While I was at college, I met some people in the lifestyle. They introduced me, and I played a little bit with them. I'm just not into public exhibition."

Colby nodded. "Some people are not, but I believe we can work around that." He didn't need her nude to play with her body. He rubbed his chin. "Before we go any further, I know you're aware I'm a Dom."

"That was obvious." She laughed and lowered her eyes. "I'm a sub, but I'm not the 24/7 type."

"Works for me. Did you play at a club or at parties?"

"Both. I should explain I was never nude, and I went to college at Berkeley. At that time, the Bay Area was more progressive than Pleasant Valley. Some of the lifestyle was pretty open." She glanced around the club. "I still can't believe the town council let Max build the club."

"I think a lot of us were surprised." He remembered when he heard about the club through the lifestyle grapevine. "Did you like the parties?"

"Some parties, I didn't like at all; others were okay."

Interesting. "What was the difference?"

"I think it had to do with who was hosting the party. Some carefully screened who they allowed in and others didn't."

"And the ones that didn't were the ones you didn't like."

She grinned. "Bingo."

"Wicked Sanctuary has an extensive vetting procedure, but even with that, sometimes someone unsuitable slips through."

"Can you tell me the vetting process?"

"Let me check." He didn't want to say anything out of line. "Be right back." Colby found Max sitting with Sierra in his lap. He paused within eye sight, not approaching until Max nodded.

"What do you need, Colby?"

"How much can I tell Lara about the vetting process?"

"I trust Lara to be discreet. You can tell her anything you want."

"Thanks, Max." Colby made his way back to Lara.

Their empty plates were gone. "Did you get rid of our plates?"

"I did."

"Thank you." He noted how she cared for everyone, even him. His heart warmed. Colby was used to taking care of himself and his mom. "Max has given me permission to discuss the vetting process with you. Would you like to move to one of the sofas to be more comfortable?"

"I'm fine here, and I can keep an eye on the food."

"All right. Those interested in joining the club go through a series of classes."

Lara tilted her head. "Classes?"

"Night one: you're given an NDA to sign, a background check approval form, and a questionnaire."

"Oh wow. I already signed an NDA, and I'm guessing the background check causes a lot of people to leave."

"More than you realize." When he joined, the first night his class had started out with fifteen people; by the end of the night, there were six of them.

"So after the first night?"

"If the background check comes back clean, it's on to class two. There you get copies of everything from the week before, and we go over the rules of the club and how to address everyone."

"Why do I have a feeling the rules are strict?"

"Not really that strict, but they're for safety and to keep certain protocols in the club."

"What kind of protocols? I saw some strange rules at the parties I attended in Berkeley."

"Not high protocol. Mainly over addressing other members, clothing, and such." Lara nodded, and Colby continued, "Class three is basically walking you through the club and explaining the equipment. The last class is an actual club night."

"What do you mean by club night?"

"Like tonight." He waved his hand. "The classes are on Thursday nights, and while the club is open, it's pretty quiet."

"I see. So the club night, is that when I make a decision on a Dom?"

"There's no timeline on you choosing a Dom." Colby leaned over. "But if you'll allow it, I'll be your Dom through the classes." He waited as Lara sat there, staring at him.

"I'd like that, Sir."

Chapter 3

The "sir" slipped off her lips naturally. Lara barely prevented herself from dropping to her knees and resting her head against Colby's hard thigh. She'd seen subs do that. It wasn't something she ever thought she'd want to do, but Colby did that to her.

"You honor me, Lara." Warm fingers touched her cheek.

Fire ran over her skin. She leaned into his touch, and his eyes sparkled with desire. Oh yes, they were compatible, at least in the minor stuff.

"I noticed when Bennett touched you earlier, you pushed him away."

"When Bennett put his hand on my arm, it didn't feel right. His touch isn't yours." That was the only way she could think of to explain it. "So how do we do this?" Lara wondered if she was crazy for even thinking about this. No, she wasn't. Her ex called her needs unhealthy and had refused even to consider her requests. She'd buried that part of herself. But with Colby, it was all coming out.

She divorced Walter four years ago—after a year of marriage. She was ready to explore once again with Colby, but she wouldn't involve her heart. She'd given it once, and that hadn't worked out too well. She'd keep it locked away.

"Do you want to go through the classes?"

"I do, and I'd like to become a member." It was quick

decision on her part. It felt right, and she wasn't going to hesitate to take what she wanted.

Colby frowned. "Have you changed your mind?"

"About what?" She tilted her head.

"Me being your Dom."

"No. I didn't mean it that way." She placed her hand over his. "I only meant I wanted to become a member so we're on even footing."

His fingers curled around hers. "You know in the club I'll be in charge."

"Of course, but outside of it, we're equals."

"Agreed."

Lara lifted her free hand to cover a yawn. "What time is it?"

"Judging by the amount of people left, somewhere around two."

"I better get home. I wonder if I should clean up or just leave it and come back tomorrow?"

"I'd say tomorrow, but I can check." He pulled her from her chair. "Be right back."

Lara watched Colby stride across the room. Damn, that man had a fine ass. Shaking her head, she made her way over to the food table. Most of the food was gone. Lara put the empty containers back into the hot boxes she'd unplugged a while ago. Taking her time, she cleaned up the area.

"You didn't need to do that," Jordan said, coming up to her with Colby.

"No trouble." Lara smiled.

"If you don't mind, why don't you leave what's on the table, and I'll drop everything off to you on Monday."

"What about the hot boxes?" She could get them loaded into her SUV and take them back to the café tomorrow.

"I'll take care of those too," Jordan said.

"Are you sure?" Lara asked. She was used to cleaning up.

"Yes." Jordan gave her a kind smile. "Go home."

"I'm not going to argue." Lara picked up the bag that held her purse. "If anything comes up, just give me a call."

Colby slipped his arm around her waist. "I'll drive you home."

"There's no need; I have my car."

"I don't want you driving alone." He stopped in the hallway. "Give me just a second." Lara waited while he slipped into the men's room. Then he was back. He'd slipped on a leather jacket over his t-shirt. "Let's go."

"Colby, there's no need for you to leave. I'm perfectly fine to drive." She didn't want him to think she was helpless.

He frowned at her. "I'm sure you are. The road is deserted this time of night, and I'd feel better if you'd allow me to drive you home. I'll make sure you have your car by tomorrow morning."

Lara let out a sigh. "Okay."

"Thank you." He kissed the back of her hand and led her over to her SUV.

"I thought you were driving?" Why were they at her vehicle?

"I am. Keys please?" He held out her hand.

She shook her head. "Sorry, I'm the only one who drives my SUV." She'd bought it right after she divorced Walter, and no one had ever driven it. She was going to keep it that way. "Why can't we go in your car?"

"Because my car is a motorcycle."

Her heart skipped a beat. "A motorcycle? Don't you

know how dangerous those are?" She slapped her hand over her mouth. It was really none of her business, and she shouldn't lecture him.

"I'm glad you care." He leaned down. "I'm very safe, and I never take chances. Keys."

"Nope." She wouldn't give in to him. "Why don't you follow me? That way we can keep an eye on each other."

He stared at her, and she held his gaze. He puffed out a breath. "All right, but you follow me. What is your address?"

A compromise she could live with. She rattled off her address, then climbed into her vehicle.

Colby was right. The roads were deserted, and because of that, it only took her twenty minutes to hit the city limits. Five minutes later, they were pulling up in front of her duplex.

"Nice area," Colby said when she climbed out of her SUV.

"Thanks." She looked at him. He was tense, and she didn't understand why. "My aunt owns them. She lives in the one on the right. I could never afford one of these places." While the café was doing well, it wasn't good enough for her to cover a mortgage on one of these duplexes. She refused to use her family's money for anything. She'd do this on her own or not at all. A shiver slipped over her skin.

"Come on. It's too cold for you to be out here." He guided her to her front door. "There's a light on inside."

"Yes. It's on a timer," she said softly. Putting her key in the door, she unlocked the deadbolt and the door lock. Once it was open, she stepped inside and disarmed the alarm system.

"Alarm?" Colby asked.

"I live alone. Makes me feel better."

"Good." His fingers ran down her cheek. "Until later, my Lara." He leaned down, and his lips brushed over hers, then he was jogging down the steps to his bike. Lara stood there, savoring the feel of his lips on hers.

He turned back and crossed his arms over his chest, staring at her. Lara shook her head and waved, then slipped inside her home, closed and locked the door. After a minute, she heard his bike roar away.

Until later, he said. She couldn't wait until Monday to see him again. Hugging herself, Lara reset the alarm and made her way to her bedroom. Soon, she'd be able to play with Colby. Excitement and nervousness warred in her mind. She'd sort them out later; right now, she wanted to enjoy the way Colby made her feel.

* * * *

Colby woke early Sunday morning, which surprised him. He'd arrived home close to three in the morning, showered, then fell into bed. Now he sat in his kitchen at eight, reading the local news on his tablet and drinking coffee.

He wondered how Lara was doing. Colby's skin itched with the need to be with her. What was so different about her? He'd been with women before, even had subs before, but Lara had called to him from the first time he saw her.

She hadn't even realized he watched her. The first time he'd walked into the café, she'd been busy refilling coffee cups. He'd ordered and sat down. From that day forward, he'd come to the café as often as he could, usually in the mornings and he'd watched her. Lara stopped at every table, chatting with everyone before going back behind the counter. She was great with people. No wonder her business was so successful. Was it any wonder he developed feelings for her?

The ringing of the intercom system broke into his thoughts. He hit the button. "Morning, Mom. Everything okay?"

"I'm fine, honey." His mother's clear voice had his shoulders slumping in relief.

He'd moved into the apartment above the garage so he could have some privacy, but he still worried about his mother, even if she was just next door. "What can I do for you?"

"What? A mother can't just call to see how her son is doing?"

Colby laughed. "Since I live next door, it seems like overkill."

"Would you be able to take me to the farmers' market today? I know you worked late last night."

"Of course." His mother was aware he'd picked up a job on the weekends; he just didn't tell her what it was. While he was pretty open with his mother, telling her he was working at a BDSM club didn't seem right. "What time do you want to leave?"

"Ten, if that's okay."

"I'll be ready." The line went dead, and Colby smiled. His mother was perfectly capable of taking care of herself, high blood pressure or not. She was only sixty. But she'd had a hard life, and it was catching up with her. His father left when Colby was still a baby, and his mother raised him alone. He didn't want her to worry about anything.

He wondered about Lara's family. While she said she couldn't afford the duplex she lived in, her aunt certainly could. But he didn't assume anything. Too many people had done that to him over the years just because he'd grown up on the poor side of town. Heck, he still lived on the edge of the area. His mother refused to move too far from their old neighborhood.

He carried his cup to the sink and then went to dress.

A little bit later, he folded his big body into his mother's compact car. She'd refused something bigger. He drove them to the farmers' market. His mother loved the market. He wandered around, keeping an eye on his mother. Then he saw someone familiar.

"Good morning, beautiful," he said softly, coming up behind her.

Lara turned her head. "Colby." Her smile widened. "What are you doing here?"

"My mother loves the market on Sundays. What about you?"

"My aunt loves it too." She glanced at an older woman talking with a florist, then the woman turned and walked over to them, a bouquet of carnations in her arms.

"Fresh flowers," her aunt said, walking up to them. "Lara, introduce me to your young man."

Lara rolled her eyes, and Colby almost laughed.

"Colby, this is my aunt, Tammy Meyer. Aunt Tammy, Colby Durham. He owns the leather store down the street from my café."

"Very nice to meet you," Colby said, holding out his hand.

"A man with manners." She placed her hand in his.

"Aunt Tammy," Lara started.

"Colby, honey." He turned to see his mother. "Mom." He took the bag from her, frowning at the weight. "Did you buy out the fruit stand?"

His mother's laugh made heads turn. "Where are my manners? I'm Martha Durham, Colby's mother."

"It's a pleasure to meet you. I'm Tammy Meyer, Lara's

aunt. Don't you just love the market?"

"Oh yes." His mother smiled, then glanced at Lara and back at him. "About time."

Before Colby could ask her what she meant, his mother turned back to Tammy. "Why don't we let these two young ones do whatever it is they do and go have some coffee?"

"I'd like that." Tammy handed Lara the flowers.

"What just happened?" Colby asked, watching the retreating figures of his mother and her aunt.

"I'm not sure." Lara looked as confused as he felt. "Should we follow them?"

"They just went into the makeshift coffee place."

"Let's join them. I could use another cup of coffee." She put her free hand over her mouth as she yawned. "Aren't you tired this morning?"

"For some reason, I woke refreshed," he said, cupping her elbow. Together, they made their way where their relatives sat at a table for four.

"I'm assuming coffee all around," Colby said as he pulled out a chair for Lara.

"Oh yes, please," his mother said.

"That would be very nice, and can you grab me a cinnamon roll?" Tammy said.

"I'll have the same," Lara said.

Colby strode away. He placed his order, waited for his number to be called, and then carried the tray to their table. His heart stuttered as he got closer.

The three women were having an animated conversation. It did his heart good to see his mother so outgoing. He worried that she was alone too much. He set the tray down and passed out the coffees. He placed a plate with a half-dozen cinnamon rolls in the middle of the table, along with smaller plates.

Lara stared at the rolls, then at him. "I hope you don't expect us to eat all that?"

His mother laughed. "You've obviously never seen Colby eat. It was a challenge to keep him fed when he was a teenager."

Tammy and his mother laughed as he sat down. "Hey, I was a growing boy."

"What's your excuse now?" Lara asked.

"I'm hungry." He snapped his teeth like a puppy going for a treat, and she laughed. God, he loved that musical sound of Lara's laugh.

"So, Martha, do you work?" Tammy asked.

Colby stiffened, and Lara shot him a questioning look.

"A bit. I like to sew, so I still do some odd jobs here and there." His mother smiled. "I enjoy it."

"That's wonderful. Sometimes, I wish I'd kept working."

"Aunt Tammy?" Lara shot her a concerned look.

"It's okay." Tammy patted Lara's hand, before looking at his mother. "My husband didn't believe in women working, so when we got married, I quit my job."

"Is he still alive?" his mother asked.

"No. He passed away young. Is your husband still alive?"

Colby drew in a sharp breath.

"I have no idea. Colby's father left me when Colby was little."

"That's horrible," Lara said, her hand reached over and touched his.

Tammy shook her head. "I have a feeling you raised a very good young man."

"Thank you." His mother blushed.

Tammy pointed at Lara. "I've told this one, while there

are some bad apples out there." Tammy turned to Lara. "Like that one you married and got rid of."

Lara groaned. "Aunt Tammy."

Tammy waved her hand. "He wasn't the right one for you, and I, for one, am glad you got rid of him. No manners, not like this one."

This time, Colby squeezed her hand. Lara's gaze met his. "That's right; you mentioned you'd been married," he said softly.

"I don't like to talk about it." She took a sip of her coffee.

Tammy shook her head. "Walter is an ass and in your father's pocket." She picked up the plate of rolls, took one, and passed the plate to his mother. Lara withdrew her hand from his as his mother held out the plate to her.

Colby took the plate from Lara, interested in what her aunt had said about her ex-husband. He'd worm the story out of her. Colby bit into his roll and let out a groan.

"These are delicious. I need the recipe," his mother said.

Tammy grinned. "I'm sure I can get that for you."

Lara's head jerked up from where she was tearing her roll apart. "Aunt Tammy." Her voice was low, and Colby was surprised at the tone.

"Don't 'Aunt Tammy' me. These are Lara's cinnamon rolls."

Colby turned to her. "You don't sell these at your café."

She shook her head. "I have an exclusive arrangement with the farmers' market for them."

"Enterprising young lady," his mother said.

"Thank you." She kept her gaze on her roll.

Was she embarrassed? She had no reason to be.

"My Colby was a crab fisherman, did you know that?" There was pride in his mother's voice.

"Really?" Tammy asked.

"Isn't that dangerous?" Lara asked, glancing at him.

"Very." He popped a piece of cinnamon roll in his mouth. Damn, this woman could cook. The dough was light with just the right amount of cinnamon and cream cheese.

"Is that all you're going to say?" Lara asked, a frown marking her features.

"Please, tell us more," Tammy said.

"Crab fishing was a lure to me. A way to make money quickly," said Colby.

"This one never worried about the danger, while I sat at home, worrying," Martha said.

Lara's frown deepened.

"Don't let her fool you. I made sure she was taken care of, and I never took chances." Colby didn't. The six years he spent in Alaska, he'd been as careful as he could be. It was a near miss on one of the crab boats that made him quit. Yes, the money was good, but he wasn't going to lose his life for some crustaceans. He had other plans. And now those plans included Lara.

"I was so glad when he came home," Martha said, patting his hand where it rested on the table. "He's such a good son. Made sure to send me money every month, and when he got home, he bought me a house."

Tammy's eyes went glassy. "That's the kind of man my Lara needs."

The groan Lara let out made all of them smile. "Okay, that's it. I'm going for a walk. Meet you at the car in thirty minutes, Aunt Tammy." Lara stood up and walked away.

"Go, young man. She won't wait for you," Tammy said.

Colby kissed his mother's cheek. "Car in thirty." Then he grabbed the bag of fruit and went after Lara. "Are you okay?" he asked when he caught up to her.

"Fine. I just don't need my aunt setting me up. She never liked my ex. That should have told me something. But no, stupid me, I married the ass."

"We all make mistakes." He didn't like the way she talked about herself.

"Maybe, but I bet you didn't marry one."

"Hey." Colby grasped her arm and pulled her to a halt. "What's going on?"

Lara shook her head as someone bumped into her.

Spying a small space between two vendors, he pulled Lara into the opening. "I know we haven't known each other for long."

Her lips tilted up. "True, yet last night I think I agreed to something I'm now not sure about."

"Is that what this is about?"

Lara looked down at her feet. "Maybe. I don't know."

Colby placed the bag between his feet, cupped Lara's chin, and lifted her face up. "All you agreed to was the classes, nothing more. If you feel you don't want to go beyond the classes, that's your decision. Everything is your decision."

"You're serious."

"Yes. You've been with people in the lifestyle; didn't they teach you about it?"

"Ummm…" Color flared in her cheeks. "Sort of."

Colby thought for a minute. "I have no expectations or requirements. I only want to be your Dom while you take the classes. After that, it's your decision. Does that work?"

"You won't get angry or upset?"

"No." He wouldn't. It would always be her decision.

"Did someone in the lifestyle get upset or angry with you because you didn't want to play with them?"

She shook her head. "You're a very different man, Colby." Her palm cupped his cheek.

"What do you mean?" He wanted to know what she saw.

"You're...what's the word I want...there's a confidence about who you are and you're not afraid of it. But there's something else. I can't find the right word."

"I'm just a man."

"You're more than that." She went up on her toes. "You're a very special man." Her lips brushed over his before she slipped from his grasp and moved away.

Colby chuckled. Lara was going to be fun to play with.

* * * *

Lara smiled as she walked through the farmers' market with Colby at her side. There was something about him. She told him he was special, and he was. Her ex would never stroll around like this. Who was she kidding? He'd never even come to a place like this.

But there was also a protective side of Colby, one that made her want to curl up into his embrace. Her lips tilted up. She didn't need a man to protect her, but there were times when it would be nice to be held and be told she was making the right decisions.

It was also obvious that Colby had a special relationship with his mother. She could only imagine what it was like growing up without a father. Lara and her father might not have gotten along well, but he'd made sure she never wanted for anything.

Maybe that was the problem. Lara didn't consider herself spoiled, but maybe she was. She spied her aunt ahead of her with Colby's mother. The two were chatting like they were old friends.

"I wonder what they're plotting," Lara said.

"Probably cooking up ways to put us in the same room together."

"Like that's a hardship." Lara liked being around Colby. That could be dangerous to her heart if she wasn't careful. They met up with the two older women, then went their separate ways at the parking lot.

"Aunt Tammy, do you think I'm spoiled?" Lara asked as she drove them back home.

"What ever gave you that idea?" Her aunt's voice sharp. "Please don't tell me Walter has been talking to you?"

Lara shook her head. "No. It was talking with Colby and his mother. I was brought up with so much, and it seems like they had so little."

"Lara, sweetie." Her aunt's voice was gentle. "You are not spoiled. Yes, you did grow up with things other children never had, but you never ever asked for anything except to go to Berkeley and not one of those stuffy colleges back east."

"Dad only allowed it because I threatened not to go at all."

"I'm glad you stood up to him, but to answer your question. You aren't like your brothers, or Walter, for that matter. Where only money matters to them, you, my sweet child, have a heart."

"Thanks, Auntie." While her aunt's words did soothe the open sore, they didn't heal it. She'd had much more opportunity than Colby. How would he feel about that if they started a relationship?

Don't put the cart before the horse, she warned herself.

When Lara got home, she put her purchases away and

then sat down and started writing out a list of pros and cons. After fifteen minutes, she realized there were more pros than cons in being with Colby. And those pros were going to make it even more difficult to guard her heart.

Chapter 4

Lara blew out a breath and waved at Eve as she left for the day. Yes, Lara was going to need more help. They'd been so busy, she barely had a second to herself and neither had Eve.

The café would close in thirty minutes, and she'd take inventory of what they needed. She was pleased with how today went. She'd smiled when a couple of the bikers had given their table to two older women during the lunch rush.

The look of surprise on the women's faces was a bit comical, reminding Lara that people needed to drop their preconceived notions. She shook her head. She was making sure the tables were clean when she heard the door behind her. She turned.

"Hi, Colby." Her heart raced and her skin tingled.

"Hey." He walked over to her. "Almost done for the day?"

"Yes, but I think you know that."

"I do." He grinned.

That grin was pure sin, and Lara wondered what he was thinking. "So what brings you here?"

"Besides you? Nothing." He took her hand in his. "I've been thinking about you all day. Are you free for dinner tomorrow night?"

"I might be." She slipped away from him to see what he would do.

"You're going to make me work for it. Okay." He followed her over to the counter. "My dear, Lara, would you please accompany me to dinner tomorrow night?"

His deep pleading tone caused her to giggle. "Don't be so melodramatic." She bopped him on the nose with her finger. "Of course I will."

The smile that crossed his lips was pure Colby. "Perfect." He glanced around.

Lara wondered why he looked around the café. It was empty.

"I'm going to kiss you now, my Lara. Is that okay?"

"Yes, please." She leaned forward.

Colby cupped the back of her neck, and his lips covered hers.

Thank goodness she was standing at the opening of the counter, so when he drew her close, there was nothing between them but air. His lips were firm and demanding against hers. Not that she minded. His kiss was that of a man who knew what he wanted.

She let herself sink against his strong chest as his tongue teased hers. The bell rang as someone walked into the café. A small cry left her lips, and he broke the kiss. Colby stepped back and released her. "Until tomorrow. I'll pick you up at seven." Then he was gone.

Lara let out a breath, watching Colby walk away

* * * *

"Dang it," Lara said as she dropped another plate. Good thing they were plastic. She'd been fumble fingers all day. Maybe because she couldn't get that kiss with Colby out of her head.

It hadn't been that long of a kiss, yet it shook her to her toes. Last night, she'd dreamed of kissing Colby over and over again, and later, the dream turned more erotic. Kissing him all over his body, to his...

"Um, Lara," Megan said.

"Huh?" Lara blinked, trying to clear her mind of her sensual dreams.

"Chicken wrap."

"Sorry." Lara grabbed a new plate and put the wrap on it. *Get with it.* The café was hopping again today. She didn't have time to let her mind wander.

By the time the lunch crowd was gone, Lara felt like she'd been working nonstop for days.

"There's my favorite café owner," Max said, walking in with Damon, each of them carrying the hot boxes.

"Thank you. I could have come out and picked them up." Jordan had called her yesterday to apologize about not bringing them to her. He'd gotten caught up in court. She'd assured him it was fine.

"Where do you want them?" Damon asked.

"In the kitchen. Follow me." She pushed aside the sliding door to the small kitchen. "Just put them under the counter, and I'll take it from there."

"I'll go get the rest of the stuff," Damon said as they walked back into the café.

"Your food was a hit Saturday night."

"I'm glad."

"I'd like to know if you'd be willing to take care of the food for the club events?" Max asked.

Lara's eyes widened. "All your events?" She hadn't even contemplated this.

"Can we sit down and talk?" He gestured to the small table against the wall.

"Sure." Lara glanced over at Megan. "Megan, I'm going to talk business with Max. Yell if you need help." Lara made her way over to the table. Max waited until she sat before he did.

"Before you get worried. We don't have a lot of parties, but last Saturday showed me that having the food was a good idea."

"You usually don't have food?"

"No. We have some snacks, like fruit and veggies, but that's about it. I like keeping the club clean."

"I can understand why." With all the equipment, along with the flooring, it made sense to keep the food to one area.

"But setting up a special corner for food with tables and chairs worked."

"Why me?"

"Why not?" Max regarded her with is hazel eyes. "Everyone loved the food you brought. It's easy to prepare and transport. Finger food, Sierra calls it. Makes it easy to eat and not a big mess."

"How often would you want me to do this?" It could be a big commitment, but she was ready to expand a bit.

"Let's start with once a month, and we'll go from there. Would that work for you?"

Damon came in with the bag and joined them at the table. "Did you ask her?"

Max laughed. "Yes."

"You did say yes, didn't you, Lara?" Damon's exuberance was like a little kid's.

"We haven't gotten there yet," Max said.

"Slowpoke," Damon said, rolling his eyes.

Lara couldn't suppress a giggle. It was interesting how these two were friends. Max seemed so serious and Damon playful. "I think we can work something out."

"Great," Max said.

"I do have a question though."

"Yes."

"I want to join the club, but I'm not sure I can afford it."

"Hot damn," Damon said.

Max glared at him.

"Okay, I'm out of here. I'll be at Colby's place." Damon jumped up and left.

"Damon gets ahead of himself sometimes." Max shook his head. "I know Colby asked to explain some things to you. The club isn't as expensive as you think. I have a class starting on Thursday night, so why don't you come out, and we can get you started."

"Okay, and yes, Colby mentioned the classes." Her life was going to get busy, but the kind of busy that made her very happy.

"Good. Seven." Max stood. "I'm glad you'll be doing the food, Lara. Everyone raved about it. See you Thursday."

Raved about it? Lara stood in shock for a moment. The food wasn't that special. At least she didn't think so. Those poor people must be in need of heartier food than the club's sliced fruit offerings. Cooking and feeding people was so second-nature to her that sometimes she forgot some people lived on snacks and convenience foods. She headed for the kitchen still reeling over the changes in her life.

"Hey, Lara, it's two forty-five," Megan said.

"Go ahead and leave." Lara stepped out of the small kitchen and waved at Megan as she left. Max's words played around in her brain. She hadn't really expected to cater more of the club's events, but it was a good thing. She looked forward to working with Max and everyone at the club. She liked everyone she'd met there, and let's face it, the club called to her like a long-lost home.

At three, Lara locked the door and finished cleaning up. She gathered up the day's receipts and put them in the safe, grabbed the money, and left by the back door. Climbing into her vehicle, she drove to the bank, which was busy, dropped off the deposit, and by the time she arrived home, it was almost five.

She had to get ready for her date with Colby. A shiver of anticipation flowed over her skin. It would be her first date in over three years. She'd tried to date right after she opened her café, but she hadn't been ready.

Once home, Lara took a quick shower and then perused her closet. What to wear tonight? Colby hadn't said where they were going. She walked over and picked up her phone from the dresser.

Lara dialed the number for Durham's leather shop instead of his cell.

"Good afternoon, this is Colby with Durham's Leather Shop. How can I help you?"

She couldn't prevent the tremor that penetrated her skin caused by his husky voice. "Hi, Colby, it's Lara. Where are we having dinner tonight?"

"Well, hi there, sweetheart. I wasn't thinking anything fancy. Is the barbecue place okay with you?"

Oh, he called her sweetheart. Wow, they hadn't even been on a date yet. The endearment warmed her heart and gave her a tingle of excitement. It implied he was serious about her already. Was that even possible? "Perfect. Now I know how to dress."

A groan came over the line.

"Please tell me you're not calling me without any clothes on."

"Well." Lara glanced down. "I guess you could consider a towel clothing."

"You're killing me here."

Lara let out a giggle. "I don't mean to. I want you alive for dinner."

"You know." His voice dropped to even a lower register. "Bad girls get punished."

Her heart fluttered with excitement. "And just what will you do to me, Sir?"

Colby's harsh breathing reached her ears. There was rustling and a muffled conversation on the other end of the line before Colby spoke again. "I think, the first thing I would do is to take you by the hand and lead you over to the bed."

Her blood heated. "Colby, you're at work."

"Technically, yes. I just stepped outside, so, where was I? Oh yes, the bed. I would slowly strip your clothes from you and place you on all fours in the middle of the bed."

Lara's breathing hitched as she backed up until her knees hit her mattress, and she flopped on the bed. "And once I'm on the bed?"

"Well, since this is a minor infraction, I would simply give you a nice spanking with my hand."

"Do you spank me hard?" Her skin tingled with anticipation.

"Oh, sweetheart, you're starting to push it. I'll give you just as much as you need."

Lara's breath caught in her throat as she closed her eyes and imagined Colby in the room with her. "Oh yes, Colby, spank me harder." She squirmed against the mattress.

She heard his exhale through the phone line. "You're liking this way too much. Let me see what else I can do to you. What did I bring in my bag?"

"Bag?"

"Of course. No good Dom is without his toy bag."

Her nipples puckered at his words. "What is in your toy bag, Sir?" Why was this phone play coming so naturally to her? Because of him.

"Now that's for me to know and for you to discover as I use my toys on you."

"Please, Sir. What will you use on me first?" Her body tingled with anticipation of what he would use on her.

"Since we don't know each other very well yet, I'll probably start with something simple. Maybe, a vibrating glove."

She hadn't heard of a vibrating glove before, but it still caused her nipples to tighten further. "What is a vibrating glove, Sir?"

"So you're not familiar with it. Interesting. It's a nice little thing that I slip over my hand and stroke up and down your body, controlling the vibrations of the glove by how hard I'm pressing on your skin."

Her pussy tightened at his words. She could almost feel his touch against her bare skin, the glove's vibrations causing her nerve endings to come alive with want and need.

"Oh please, Sir." Her voice was breathless.

"I will please you, but not until later, my naughty sub."

The slamming of a door brought Lara back to earth, hard. What a fantasy. Or was it? They were going to dinner tonight, and who knew what could happen afterward?

"Damn, I gotta go. Until later."

The line went dead, and Lara laid there, her body pulsing with need. It wouldn't take much to push her over the edge. Her fingers flirted with the edge of her towel. No. She wouldn't get herself off, not right now. She wanted to keep all of this for Colby.

Lara climbed off the mattress and went back over to her closet. She pulled out a pair of designer jeans and a flirty top. Maybe she'd make Colby work for her consent, but she kind of doubted it. She was ready for anything he could throw at her.

Chapter 5

Colby climbed the steps to Lara's front door. His cock pulsed with each step he took. After their phone call this afternoon, his dick had stayed hard. Colby knocked on the door, and a second later, the door opened to reveal a smiling Lara.

His gaze ran over her from head to toe. The brightly colored top clung to her breasts, and he would have sworn she'd been poured into those jeans. "You look so delicious I could eat you for dinner."

Lara smiled shyly. "Well, you did say casual. Do you want to come inside?"

His cock jumped, and he closed his eyes for a moment. "Better not tempt fate right now." He held out his hand.

"Okay." She reached back, grabbed her purse, and set the alarm before she put her hand in Colby's, closing the door behind her as she walked out onto the stoop.

"Before we go." He leaned closer to her. "I know we haven't officially agreed to a relationship, so let me rectify that right now. I need verbal consent that you're willing for me to be your Dom in and out of Wicked Sanctuary."

Her eyes widened before her lashes fell. Colby waited. He wasn't going to rush her, but he needed that consent. While they'd had pretty basic phone sex today, once he had her consent, he'd take it up a notch.

"I believe I could agree to that." Her voice was soft.

"I need a little more than that. Yes or no."

Her lashes rose, and she tilted her head back until their gazes met. "Yes, Sir."

His cock pulsed against his jeans. "Thank you, sweetheart." He ran his finger over her cheek. "We have a lot to talk about over dinner."

"Like what?"

"Your level of experience in the lifestyle. Plus other things." Colby guided her down the steps to his motorcycle. He frowned. That top wasn't going to keep her warm on his bike.

Opening the small storage compartment on his bike, he pulled out a leather jacket. It would be a little big on her, but until he could get her something that fit, it would work. He shook out the jacket and held it out to her.

Lara slipped her arms into the jacket, and Colby turned her around and zipped up the front. Then he grabbed the extra helmet and put it on her head. She shifted from one foot to the other.

"I can't believe I get to ride with you on your bike," she said, excitement tingeing her voice.

Her enthusiasm pleased him. "The jacket's a little big, but it'll keep you warm. You'll have to come by the shop so I can get you one that fits you better."

"Do you think I'll need one?"

Colby grinned at her. "Most definitely." He slipped on his helmet. "The helmets are equipped with Bluetooth so we can talk."

"That's so cool."

He helped her onto the bike and then he mounted. Colby started the engine. "Put your arms around my waist. I'm not going to go too fast."

"But I want to go fast."

"After a few rides, once you get used to it, I'll take you out for a real run." Her arms slid around his waist, and his dick pulsed. It was going to be a long night if he couldn't get his body under control.

Colby released the brake, and they were off. Lara's arms tightened, and he enjoyed the feel of her body pressed against his. As promised, he kept it slow and easy, and all too soon, they pulled up to the barbecue place.

Colby parked the bike and helped Lara off. When he took her helmet off, she was grinning from ear to ear as she ran her fingers through her hair.

"That was fun."

"I'm glad you liked it." Colby stored her helmet with his before taking her hand and leading her up the walkway. The restaurant was busy for a Tuesday evening. He walked up to the hostess with a smile.

"Colby, it's so good to see you again," the blonde woman said before leaning over and kissing his cheek. "I have your table ready, just follow me."

Colby gestured for Lara to precede him, and he noted the questioning look in her eyes. They had one of the best tables in the house. It was his favorite table. Next to the windows where, during summer, you could see the ducks out on the pond.

"Mike will be with you shortly. Enjoy your dinner." The hostess set the menus on the table and bounced away.

Colby held Lara's chair out for her. She hesitated for a second then sat down. He took the seat next to her rather than across. For what he wanted to discuss, it would work better if they were close to each other.

"The hostess seemed to know you," she said, her voice cool.

"I've known Tina since she was in diapers. She and her

mom lived down the street. We grew up together." Her jealousy warmed his heart, and he didn't blame Lara for questioning him. He'd probably do the same.

"Oh." She looked down at the table.

Colby took her hand and lifted it to his lips. "Tina isn't a threat. She's just an old friend. I want you to understand that. I have a lot of friends from the neighborhood."

"I bet a lot of women."

"Yes." His lips caressed her knuckles. "But there's only one woman with me tonight. And that's you."

"I have no reason to act jealous."

"You have every right. I just asked you to be in a relationship with me. That's the reason this dinner is so important. To get to know each other better." He rubbed his thumb over the back of her hand.

Lara's lips fluttered in a smile.

"Are we okay?" he asked.

"We are." She tugged her hand from his hold and began looking over the menu. "So many choices."

Her acceptance of their relationship warmed him. "Much like your café. I always have trouble choosing."

"But you pick the same thing. Every day."

"Because it's easier that way." He looked at her over his menu. "Would you like me to order for you?"

Lara was silent for a moment, then she closed her menu and set it down in front of her, folding her hands on top of it. Colby prepared himself for a tongue lashing. What was he thinking? She knew food and was an independent woman. "Thank you for asking. I actually like that idea. Less for me to think about right now."

Colby's Dom side preened at her words. He wasn't an expert in the lifestyle, not by a long shot. But Max had once told him he had good instincts, and tonight, he was going with those instincts.

When their waiter arrived, Colby gave their dinner order, and ordered a beer for himself. He looked over at Lara, and she grinned and told the waiter she'd have a beer also.

"So, how do we go about this?" she asked.

Colby stretched his arm out and rested it behind her on her chair. "We get to know each other. I know a little bit about you already."

"And what do you know?" Her brows came together, not exactly in a frown, but as if she was concentrating hard on something.

"You have a close relationship with your aunt. You love your business. And you're interested in the lifestyle."

She shook her head. "There's a lot more to me."

"I know there is. So, tell me, Lara, how does one who grows up with a rich family end up owning a café and living next door to her aunt?"

* * * *

Well, damn. It wasn't like Lara had hidden that part of her life, but she didn't talk about it. A lot of people treated her differently when they found out she came from money. But Colby seemed different. Guess she'd find out. "How long have you known?" Her heart clenched.

"Since the beginning."

She looked up as the waiter brought their beers and then disappeared. "Does it bother you?" She hadn't realized that Colby knew about the family name. It wasn't like Meyer was all that different, but growing up in Pleasant Valley, most people were aware of her family's money. Theirs. Not hers.

"Does it bother you that I grew up on the poor side of town?"

"Of course not. Why would it?" Where he grew up had no bearing on their relationship.

"Why should your upbringing bother me?"

Lara stared at him. "Some men are intimidated by the money my family has. Others just see me as a meal ticket." Walter had seen her as that and more. Well, he'd gotten his wish, but not the way he thought.

Colby took a sip of his beer and set the mug down. "Is that what your ex did? He saw you as a get-rich-quick scheme?"

"Pretty much." She wasn't going to lie to Colby.

"So how did you meet him?"

"At Berkeley." Lara took a drink of her own beer. "I met Walter when I was a junior. We got along, and he was fun to be with." That was the truth, at least in the beginning.

"What did you study at Berkeley?"

"I studied how to be an entrepreneur. Are you sure you want to hear this?" Her life wasn't that exciting.

Colby shifted in his chair, his fingers dancing over her shoulder. "I do. This is a part of you. To make this work, I need to know."

Lara sat there a bit stunned. "Before we get into my life, explain a little bit more to me about the lifestyle."

"From what you told me Saturday night, you played a little bit while you were at Cal Berkeley. Were you ever in a long-term relationship with someone in the lifestyle?"

"No. I attended some parties and visited a club a few times. But it was always with friends, and there was never anything romantic between us."

"Was there anything like what you saw at Wicked Sanctuary on Saturday?"

Lara tilted her head. "Yes and no. The only equipment was really X frames and some spanking benches. Nothing like I saw on Saturday." She closed her eyes and thought back to those times. "Saturday, I don't know. Everyone seemed to be having fun. There didn't seem to be a lot of drama going on." Some of the parties she'd attended had so much drama going on, she hadn't stayed.

"I'm not going to say there isn't drama. There has been. But that's why the club has a vetting process."

"Max mentioned that today. I'm a little nervous about it."

Colby caressed her shoulder. "What are you nervous about? I can't see you having anything in your past that would stop you from becoming a member."

"It's just…my family." She let out a sigh. "They never wanted me to open the café; they thought it was beneath the family name." She wasn't about to use her married name. She dumped that as soon as the divorce papers were filed.

"That's their problem."

"Yeah, it is, but sometimes, it's also mine. You saw my brother and my ex last week and the ruckus they made."

"Let me ask you this: Would you have been happy going to work at the bank with your father and brothers?"

A shudder went through Lara's body. "Lord no. While I'm good at running my café, there's a reason I hired an accountant. Numbers are not my thing."

"There's your answer. One thing I've learned over the years is not to let family define me. My father left when I was two. My mother worked several jobs to keep a roof over our heads and food on the table. I'll never forget the lessons she taught me."

Lara turned in her chair. "From what I've seen, she raised a very caring man." She ran her fingers over his jaw, enjoying the feel of his skin against hers. "You've done so much with your life. I feel like I've just stagnated here in

Pleasant Valley."

"Hey." He gripped her chin and turned her face toward him. "You've not stagnated. Pay attention tomorrow at the café, and by that, I mean really look at the people who come in, the way the people interact with you. You don't care about their backgrounds. You don't care about where they came from. You're happy they're there, and you make sure they're happy."

"Of course. I'm happy I have customers."

Colby laughed. "Honey, you'd be just as happy if you only had two customers. Let me put this another way: Look at the way you treat the bikers. Have you ever noticed how others shift away from them?"

Lara frowned. "Yes, and I don't like it. But I can't stop others."

"There's the difference. You care."

"I do. I hadn't thought of it like that." She hadn't, not in a long time.

Colby opened his mouth, but the waiter approached the table carrying two plates. He placed one in front of each of them.

"Wow, there's enough food here to feed a family of ten." The laughter in her voice made him smile.

"Maybe not a family of ten, but remember, we will need to keep our strength up."

Her nipples puckered at his words. "Hmmm, maybe you will, but I think I have more than enough stamina for you." Where were these flirty words coming from? She'd never flirted with Walter like this. Maybe because Walter didn't have a flirty side? He was, after all, a stuffy banker.

Colby stared at her. "You're playing with fire, sweetheart."

"Maybe I don't mind getting burned." Oh man, she was

going over the top here.

His eyes flared with desire. "If we weren't in a public place…" He let his words trail off, but Lara got their meaning.

She squirmed in her chair but kept a smile on her face. They were going to have fun together. She was excited to get started.

Lara froze. When had she last let herself be herself? Not since she met Walter, at least. She'd hidden a part of herself, and she didn't have to do that with Colby. Colby liked being with her the way she was.

"So how did you start working at the club?" Lara asked.

"I was asked. I'm not sure how much you know about the club."

"I'm aware that Max, Jordan, and Damon are all partners."

"Yes. They asked me if I would step in to help, since they now all have women in their lives."

"Why would that make a difference?"

"You'll learn this in your first class, but when you get through all your classes and are allowed into the club as a member, you need someone to show you the ropes. Since some people come in as singles, there needs to be a mentor/trainer."

Lara put her fork down and stared at Colby. "Okay, I can see why they would ask for help. I can't see any of the Doms' girlfriends being happy about them mentoring anyone, though." She shook her head. "Girlfriend is a tame word for Sierra, Crystal, and Tessa."

"They are forces to be reckoned with." Colby laughed. "They take their relationships seriously. Like they should."

"Is that why you asked me to be in a relationship?" She

wondered why he asked her.

"I asked you because I wanted to. It doesn't matter if you're a member of the club or not, Lara."

"So if I wasn't interested, you'd give up the club?" He was full of surprises.

"No." He reached over and took her hand. "I want you to understand, this is a part of me. I'm not heavily into BDSM, but I enjoy it. It's an outlet for energy and a sensual high."

"I'm not sure I understand it all, at least not yet. But I'm glad I get to explore with you and only you."

"That makes me very happy." He squeezed her hand before releasing it. "Would you please tell me more about your ex-husband?"

Lara closed her eyes for a second then opened them. While she hated talking about her ex, Colby deserved to know. "As I mentioned, I met him at Berkeley. We dated and had fun together, but there was always something missing."

"If you knew something was missing, why did you marry him?"

She thought for a moment before she answered him. "You know it's really sad to say, but I married him to get my family off my back." She rubbed her temple. "My family really liked Walter, and it took pressure off me and let me pursue what I wanted to do. Looking back, it was a stupid thing to do."

Colby's head jerked in her direction. "You were not stupid." He enunciated each word. "You did what you had to do at the time. It seemed like your only option."

"Nevertheless, it was a mistake from the first." She shook her head. "Can we discuss something else, please?"

"One last question. Was your ex ever into kink?"

"No. Walter didn't like anything but the missionary position, and trust me, that gets old fast."

Colby grinned. "It does. And I can guarantee I do more than just missionary."

Her body heated. Colby did that to her and so much more. Walter had his uses, but Colby… He called to her. He touched a place inside her that she'd hidden from the world. Even from herself.

"So have you ever been married?"

Laughter filled his eyes. "No, I haven't. I've never really come close."

"And why is that? You're handsome guy. The women should be all over you." It had surprised her that he wasn't attached.

"I'm not going to say there haven't been women in my life. Just not anyone I wanted to spend the rest of my life with."

Lara thought about his words for a few moments as she ate. "I don't blame you. So, if you haven't had someone special in your life, who did you play with at the club?"

"The club has what they call club subs. These are women who are in the lifestyle and like to play."

"So none of them are in a committed relationship?"

"Actually, a couple are."

"How does that work?" When she was at Berkeley, she'd seen some open relationships but not open marriages.

"Polygamous relationships are not at all unusual in the lifestyle. The thing is that society hasn't caught up to the lifestyle; we're definitely ahead of the times."

"I hadn't thought about it like that. It seems so very difficult to keep everyone in the loop."

"Another thing about the lifestyle—communication is very important. Actually, it comes in second, consent is the most important."

"That makes sense. How could you fully trust someone with your body if you haven't been honest and communicated with them?" When she'd tried to be honest with her ex, it had blown up in her face. So she'd buried her needs. No wonder her marriage fell apart so fast.

"Correct. I could be wrong, but I suspect what you saw in college was people attempting to be in the lifestyle. They didn't hold to open, honest communication. And possibly, consent was a wobbly hill."

Lara sat there for a moment and thought about her time in college. Colby was right; there wasn't much talk about communication, or honesty for that matter. Those she'd hung out with believed in consent, but based on what she knew now, they were only dabbling in kink.

"You're right."

"There's a couple of the club subs that are in committed relationships, but they are very open and honest with their partners. Heck, their partners sometimes come to our private parties. Not to play, but to socialize. To understand their partner and to help themselves understand what their partner needs."

"That's interesting. But how do they handle…sex?"

"The lifestyle isn't all about sex. It's about a connection. A connection between play partners, one so deep that the partners feed off of each other."

"I'm not sure I understand." She'd never seen a connection like he was talking about. She'd read about it in the romance books but didn't think it was anything but part of the fantasy.

"You will. Let's get you through the classes first, and you'll understand more."

"I think I can do that." She could do it with Colby by

her side to guide her.

"I'll be with you the entire time. We're in this together until you say we're not." He gestured to her plate. "Now eat up, or you won't get dessert."

Lara blinked at Colby. Was he was saying he was committed to her until she said it was over? It was so unexpected. "I don't know if I'll have enough room for dessert." She fluttered her eyelashes. "But I think you're talking about something much different than a sweet treat."

"You won't know until later."

Lara couldn't help smiling as she went back to eating. She was looking forward to the dessert Colby promised her.

Chapter 6

Three hours later, Colby pulled up to Lara's duplex. She'd eaten so much at dinner dessert wasn't even a possibility. But she wouldn't trade that dinner for anything in the world. She'd gotten more out of Colby about his childhood and how he'd protected the young girls in his community.

Tina was one of those girls. Colby had made sure that she was safe from the gangs that roamed the neighborhood, and when it was time, he'd helped her get a job and get into college. This man had many facets to him, and she was looking forward to exploring each one.

He walked her up the steps to her front door. He cupped her shoulders and turned her back to him once she'd opened the door and turned off her alarm.

"Thursday is the first class. I'll be there when the class starts at seven, so don't worry if you get there early and I'm not there."

"I'm looking forward to it." She was. A new chapter in her life.

"Good. As for tonight, I know you're full, but here's my dessert." He lowered his head, and his lips captured hers.

Lara closed her eyes and gave herself over to his kiss, firm lips against her soft ones. His warm body pressed against hers. She slipped her arms around his waist and pulled him even closer as he cupped the nape of her neck.

When his tongue traced her lips, Lara opened her mouth. Their tongues dueled and danced around each other. She tasted a slight hint of the coffee they had after dinner. She didn't want to let him go. Should she invite him in?

Colby pulled back and gazed down at her. Lara wanted to drown in the desire she saw in his eyes.

"Do you want to come in?" Her voice was soft.

"Not tonight, sweetheart." His hand tightened on her neck. "We both have work tomorrow, and it's too soon for us."

Disappointment flowed through Lara's veins, but he was right. "Until Thursday then?"

"You know you'll see me tomorrow. I can't go without my daily fix." His fingers caressed the back of her neck before he released her. "Inside now, sweetheart. I'll see you tomorrow."

Lara slipped inside, closed the door, and threw the deadbolt. With her back against the door, she slid down to sit on the floor and basked in the warm fuzzies. She waited until she heard Colby's motorcycle start and then until the sound of the engine faded away before she forced herself to stand. Setting the alarm, Lara made her way to her bedroom.

She'd see him tomorrow and in class on Thursday. Her life was about to become very interesting. Stripping out of her clothing, she realized she still had the leather jacket Colby gave her. She'd give it back to him tomorrow. Or maybe she'd keep it until she got one of her own. She buried her nose in the jacket, and remembered being wrapped around Colby with the wind rushing through her hair. The rumble of the bike under her and her blood soaring through her veins.

A smile crept over her lips. Maybe she'd find some time, check out Colby's shop, and get herself a nice leather jacket. She was curious about his shop, and it was the perfect opportunity to see Colby again.

* * * *

Colby unlocked the door to his shop and began to walk around the store. He made mental notes of items that were running low. When the door opened, he turned.

"Well, good morning, beautiful. What brings you here?" He was happy to see Lara; he just hadn't expected to see her in his store.

"I come bearing gifts." She held up a cup of coffee and a white bag.

"You're a lifesaver." He'd texted her this morning that he was running late so he wouldn't be over to the café until later. Leave it to her to bring him his morning coffee.

"I wouldn't want you to fall asleep on the job." She walked over to the counter and set his coffee and bag down. "Besides I've been wanting to come in and see your shop."

"Curious are we?"

"You bet I am. I've been so busy with the café and the classes at the club over the last few weeks that I haven't had time until today."

Lara was doing fantastic at the classes. She seemed curious and willing to explore, so he couldn't have asked for a better partner.

"Did you finally get through all your interviews for new hires?" Colby took the lid off and inhaled, closing his eyes in bliss. The heavenly smell of deep, rich coffee woke him up almost as much as Lara's smile.

"Yes, I finally did. I have at least four potential employees. Now I have to narrow the field."

"You're not going to hire all four?" Colby opened the

bag and peeked in, distracted by its contents. He pulled out the white wrapper and set it on the napkin. Slowly he opened it and stared. "Okay, what is this?"

Lara's laughter floated through the air. "I don't need four new people, and it's a new sandwich I'm trying out. Take a bite, and tell me what you think."

Colby stared at the sandwich. He saw ham and cheese, but what else was there? With a shrug of the shoulders, he lifted up the sandwich and took a bite.

The saltiness of the ham and bacon mixed in with the spicy tang of sausage hit his tongue, then the sharp cheddar cheese along with the milder Swiss made itself known. He chewed and swallowed.

"This is great," he said.

"Thank you." Lara moved around the shop, stopping every so often. "The bread is a slightly toasted artesian sourdough."

Colby took another bite and then another. "How did you come up with this one?"

"I thought about what you said, last week. About how some people want more protein. I figured I'd start with this, and for those who don't want the carbs, I can put it in a lettuce wrap."

"I think this is going to be a big hit. What are you going to call it?" He kept his gaze on her as he polished off the sandwich and finished his coffee.

"I'm not sure yet." Lara stood by the women's jackets. He watched her pull one off and try it on.

The jacket fit a heck of a lot better than the one he'd loaned her. Colby made note of which jacket she was trying on so, when she put it back, he could take it off the rack and give it to her as a present.

He kept his gaze on her as she put the jacket back and

then wandered around the store. She paused by the sign that said, *21 and over*. "Go take a look," he encouraged. They'd walked around the club last Thursday as part of her last class. She didn't flinch at anything she saw and even asked lots of questions. He'd never get tired of giving her answers.

"And just what am I going to find?"

"I don't want to spoil the surprise." He kept his gaze on her until she shrugged her shoulders and slipped into the partitioned off area. Colby turned as the door opened. "Morning, Kase."

"Morning, boss. I'll put my stuff in the office and get to work."

"No problem." Colby moved out from behind the counter. "I'll be in the adult area. Holler if you need me."

Kase waved his hand and disappeared into the office. Colby went over to the sectioned area for adults only. He stepped inside to see Lara standing by the row of floggers.

"See something you like?" She looked delicious in his store.

Lara spun around, her hand going to her heart. "You scared me."

"I figured you'd hear me come in." It wasn't like he'd been quiet. "So what do you think?" He gestured around the room.

"Interesting." She touched one of the floggers, her fingers lightly caressing the falls. "Do you make these yourself?"

"Some of them, yes." His gaze followed her as she went over to the fet wear. "I have people asking me for special orders, and I enjoy creating something different."

"I bet."

Colby kept his gaze on her. "Since tomorrow night is

our night at the club, do you have something to wear?"

"Not yet." She glanced at the leather skirts.

"Why don't you pick something out and try it on?"

Her startled gaze met his. "Try it on?" Her voice had a slight tremor to it.

"Yes. I have dressing rooms."

She turned back to the display of skirts, her fingers gliding over the soft leather. "I think," she paused as if gathering her thoughts. "Yes, I'd like to try one on."

One of the things he'd learned over the past few weeks about Lara: When she committed herself to something, she committed her whole self. There was no holding back. There might be some hesitation, but that was normal. Compared to her previous, almost superficial experience with the lifestyle, what he and Lara were exploring was new to her.

He watched her pick up three different skirts before turning to him.

"Show me the dressing room, please. I need to do this quickly and get back to the café. I left Eve alone."

"Let's go." He led her out of the adult area and across the store to the dressing rooms. "Will you model for me?"

Her cheeks turned pink before she turned and slipped into the dressing room. "Maybe." Lara pulled the curtain closed, and Colby smiled. He loved teasing her.

He waited, a little bit impatiently, as she tried on the skirts. He could hear the wrestling of clothing. After several minutes, Colby knocked on the wood frame. "Are you coming out so I can see?"

"Nope." There was laughter in her voice.

"Come on. I really want to see what they look like." There was a rustle of clothing, and minutes later, the curtain was pulled back. "Too bad." She held the skirts out to him.

"They really didn't work. At least not for me."

"Too bad." He wondered if the fit was wrong, or did she have a body image problem?

"Yes, it was." Her voice was soft, and she leaned close to him. "See you later." She brushed a kiss over his cheek before she stepped around him and left his store.

Colby shook his head and carried the leather skirts over to the cleaning table. As he wiped them down, he noted the sizes. He made an educated guess on which size would fit Lara.

Kase was behind the register. "What do you need me to do today, boss?"

"Take inventory. We were pretty busy yesterday, and I want to make sure we have enough product."

"You got it."

After he finished cleaning the skirts, Colby returned them to their spots. He pulled the leather jacket from the rack and then stood there staring at the leather clothing. An idea popped into his head, and he walked over to Kase.

"I'm going to be in my workroom if you need me."

"All right."

Colby made his way to his workroom. He usually only worked at night or on weekends, but he wanted to work on this idea now.

* * * *

Lara stared at the box like it was a snake waiting to bite her. She plucked the note from under the ribbon and tore the envelope open.

Lara, after you left the store yesterday, an idea came to mind. I hope you like this. See you tonight. Don't forget; I'm picking you up at seven. Colby.

Gathering her courage, she pulled the ribbon and lifted the white lid off the box to reveal white tissue paper.

Carefully, she parted the paper and stared at the clothing below.

Her fingers trembled as she lifted the material from the box. Her breath caught in her throat. How did he know?

While Lara wasn't an exhibitionist, she was well aware of the club rules on clothing. Colby as well.

She held the up the first piece of material. A halter top made of leather that laced up in the front. She carefully laid it on her bed and picked up the second clothing item. A leather skirt.

Yes, she tried a couple on in Colby's shop, but she'd found them either too short or little too restrictive, and she couldn't quite move the way she wanted to. But this one… Her fingers caressed the supple, buttery-soft black leather.

Lara blew out a breath. How was she to play this? These last few weeks, she and Colby had gone out to dinner a few times and to the classes at the club. He hadn't pressured her for sex or even play. Tonight was their first night to play in the club if she choose to. She laid the skirt aside and put the box in her closet. Was she really going to wear what he'd sent her? She didn't know yet, but it wouldn't hurt to try it on.

She quickly stripped down to her underwear. Removing her bra, she slipped on the halter top and laced up the front. It wasn't as stiff as she thought it might be. The built-in bra cupped her breasts and lifted them.

One down. Picking up the skirt, Lara held it up. This looked different than the ones she tried on in his shop. She slipped the skirt on and pulled it up. It was snug around her waist and framed her hips well.

She walked around her bedroom before stopping in front of her full-length mirror. Was that really her? Her cheeks were full of color; her blue eyes sparkled. She twisted and turned, keeping her gaze on the mirror.

While she had done a lot of reading over the last few weeks and talked with Sierra, Crystal, and Tessa, nothing prepared her for how she felt right now.

Lara had never considered herself beautiful. Passable, yes. But in this outfit… She felt sexy and beautiful. How did Colby know what she didn't know? The man had unknown depths to him, and she was looking forward to exploring each and every one.

Shoes. She learned a long time ago she didn't like heels, but the club had strict rules. She couldn't really see herself going barefoot. Wait a second, she remembered reading something about… Darn it, she couldn't remember.

Walking over to her dresser, she picked up her cell phone and texted Sierra. Within a few minutes Sierra texted her back a note with a picture. Lara looked at the picture first. That's it. Ballet flats. Okay. She thanked Sierra and started rummaging through her closet and unearthed a pair of red ballet slippers.

These would work. But there was one more thing. She went back to her dresser and opened the drawer. Regular panties wouldn't work tonight. She'd need something different.

She took off her normal underwear and slipped on a thong. She'd bought them on a whim but hadn't worn them more than once because they were uncomfortable. They didn't call it butt floss for nothing. Lara consolidated the other items she would take with her tonight into a small purse, excitement flowing through her veins. She was glad the club had lockers for them to put their belongings in, since purses weren't allowed on the club floor.

Once that was done, Lara slipped on the ballet slippers and walked into her living room.

She had about ten minutes before Colby was to arrive. Oh wait, she needed a coat. There was no way she could walk around like this let alone… Maybe she better drive tonight.

There was no way she could ride Colby's bike in the skirt. Opening the hall closet, she pulled out her long raincoat. Her doorbell rang. She looked out and saw Colby standing there.

She slipped her coat on. Something inside her wanted to surprise Colby. After buttoning the garment closed, she opened the door.

The disappointment on Colby's face was priceless. "Did my gift not work?"

Lara's lips turned up. "You'll just have to wait and see."

His eyes flared with desire. "Are you sure you want to tease me this way?"

She shifted from one foot to the other. "Since this is the only time tonight I'm going to be able to do this, yes." Once they were in the club, he was in charge. A tremor of anticipation flowed through her veins.

"You and I are going to have fun." He leaned over and brushed a light kiss over her lips. "Ready to go?"

"Yes, but I was wondering if I should drive. I don't think I can ride your bike in this outfit."

"No worries." He gestured to the small green SUV sitting in front of her duplex. "I borrowed one of Damon's vehicles. I knew it would be difficult for you to ride my bike. We'll work something out so you won't have to worry next time."

Colby guided her down the steps and into the vehicle. Feeling a little devilish, Lara allowed her raincoat to part and show her legs as she climbed in. Colby caressed the inside of her knee as he pulled the fabric back into place. "Just wait till we get to the club," he said, his voice husky.

He closed the door, and Lara put on her seatbelt. Her skin tingled from his brief touch. "So, what are we going to do tonight?"

"It depends on what you want." Colby expertly drove through town and out toward the club. "Since this is your first night in the club after the classes, I figured we would at least walk around and watch some of the scenes together and discuss which ones you'd like to try." He reached across and entwined his fingers with hers. "There's no rush and no pressure. Tonight is to get you comfortable being in the club."

Lara thought for a moment. "What if I would like to try something tonight?"

"We will discuss it, and I will decide if you're ready to try it or not."

She frowned at him. "You will decide?"

"As your Dom, it is my responsibility to make sure not only that you are safe, but that you're not jumping ahead into something you're not ready for. I don't want you to run screaming from the club."

"If I was going to run screaming, I would've done it by now." Nothing she'd seen so far made her afraid; if anything, it made her excited.

"Remember, I read your questionnaire. There are some hard limits on there."

"True. But I wouldn't pick one of those."

"I didn't think you would, but what about being bound to the wheel, nude, and having me flog you with a cat o'nine tails?"

She let out a sigh. "Since being nude is a hard limit, you won't violate that. But I get it. I would not be ready for the other things you mentioned." A tiny icy finger ran up her spine. She trusted Colby, and she trusted Max and the others in the club. She'd watched the night she catered the party and throughout the classes. Everyone seemed at ease with everyone else, and the dungeon monitors watched everything. "Don't you have to work tonight?"

"Just from eight to ten. Jordan is going to take my ten to twelve shift."

"That's nice of him."

"He understood that we'd want time together tonight."

Lara glanced out the window and watched the trees as they drove by. She was excited, yet a little apprehensive. Her emotions were all over the place tonight. She was going to push her own boundaries tonight.

A little bit later, Colby parked outside the club. There were only a few cars. "We're a little early, but I wanted to give you time to do whatever you needed to do before you're ready to enter the club."

"Thank you." He helped her from the car, and together, they walked inside. Ralph signed them both in and handed Lara a new wristband. This one was purple and white.

"What do I do with my old one?" She'd worn it during her classes but that had been it.

"I'll check with Max, but if you give it to me, I can make sure it's cleaned and is as good as new." Colby guided her down the small hallway and stopped outside the ladies' bathroom. "If I'm not here when you're ready to go into the club, just let Ralph know, and he'll come find me."

"All right." He released her hand, and Lara walked into the ladies' room. A smile tilted her lips as she walked in. This was so much more than the ladies' room. There were showers, heated towels, benches to sit on, and of course, the lockers. She'd been amazed when she first saw it.

"Oh good, you're here," Sierra said.

"It's so good to see you." Lara walked over and embraced Sierra. "Thank you for helping me out earlier."

"No problem. I love the red." Sierra gestured to her shoes.

"They were the only ones I had." She moved over to one of the lockers and set her purse inside, then unbuttoned her raincoat, slipped it off, neatly folded it, and put it into the locker.

"Holy heck," Sierra said. "Has Colby seen you yet?"

Lara locked the locker and turned to Sierra. "Not yet. Do you think he's going to like it on me? He made it." Lara was proud of Colby's leather skills.

"Lara, he's going to be corralling all the Dom's tonight. Good thing you're wearing a purple and white wrist band."

"Is it too much?" She hadn't thought about how other men would see her. Maybe this wasn't such a good idea.

"It's perfect," Sierra said, touching her on the shoulder. "I know we're more acquaintances than friends, but I'll sit with you tonight while Colby is working. That way, you're not alone, and you can ask me any questions you want."

"Sierra, I do consider you a friend. You came into the café shortly after I opened it. And later, you brought your friends."

"That makes me happy."

"Oh good, Lara can join our group," Tessa said, walking into the room.

"Group?"

"Yes," Sierra said. "For years, it's just been the three of us. Tessa, Crystal, and me. But since we've now all started coming to the club, we're open to expanding our girl group."

"That sounds like fun." Lara had never had a lot of girlfriends. She looked forward to spending time with the women.

"Great," Tessa said, stripping off the long coat she wore. "You need to join us for book club night as well."

Lara blinked. Why hadn't she heard of any of this stuff before? Maybe because she'd been concentrating on her business. But the idea of a women's book club sounded very intriguing. "When do you meet?"

"First Wednesday of the month, usually," Tessa said, turning around.

Lara's eyes grew wide. While Sierra was dressed in boy shorts and a baby doll top, Tessa wore a skirt that barely covered her butt and a pretty purple bra. Lara almost felt overdressed.

"Where do you meet?"

"Kleinman's."

"Isn't that the adult store?" Lara remembered hearing something about it over a month ago.

"Yep." Tessa smiled. "Damon owns it."

Lara blinked. Oh yeah, that had been mentioned in the article she'd read after the press conference.

"We better get going," Sierra said. "You know the guys get impatient, and they might storm the bathroom to find us."

"One of these days," Tessa said, rolling her eyes before linking her arm through Lara's.

Sierra linked her arm through Lara's other arm. "Let's go surprise our men."

Arm in arm, the three of them walked out of the ladies' room. Lara's confidence soared.

Chapter 7

Colby paced the small hallway while Max and Damon watched him. Both men had big grins on their faces.

"You haven't even played with her and already you've fallen," Max said.

Colby stopped and stared at Max. "I'm not sure I've fallen or anything like that yet." He was attracted to Lara, and he'd like nothing more than to have her in his bed. But fallen?

Movement caught his attention, and he turned toward the ladies' room. Three women walked out. His gut clenched when he saw Lara.

He never envisioned how she would look in the clothing he'd made. The halter top cupped her breasts and lifted them, making his mouth water with all her exposed creamy skin.

The just-above-the-knee length leather skirt clung lovingly to her hips, and he was sure to her ass as well. The red slippers she wore gave the outfit a splash of color and made him think that there was fire—hot, hot fire—beneath the calm, cool exterior Lara showed everyone.

The next thing he knew, he was standing in front of her, not even realizing he'd moved. Sierra and Tessa had stepped aside. Colby stared at her. "I may have said this before or maybe not. But you take my breath away. You are so fucking beautiful."

Her skin flushed, and she ducked her head. "Thank you, Sir."

The *sir* had his dick pulsing and pushing against khakis. If this kept up, he wouldn't be able to hide his erection. Not that it mattered in the club, but he didn't want to make Lara uncomfortable. He was vaguely aware of their friends striding away. "I'm going to have you sit in the green area while I work."

"That's fine, Sir. Sierra said she would keep me company and answer any questions I have."

"Good. Just remember who you belong to."

"And who is that, Sir?"

He saw the twinkling amusement in her eyes and could not hold back his own grin. "You belong to me. Until you tell me you don't."

"Of course, Sir."

He drew her arm through his, and they walked into the club. Heads turned, and Colby glared at the men, who hastily turned away. A soft giggle reached his ears, and he looked down at Lara.

"Don't scare everyone tonight, Sir."

"Witch." Colby led her over to the green area. Sierra and Tessa were already waiting there. The Neanderthal in him wanted to stake a claim, and Colby didn't blame him.

He curved his hand around the back at Lara's neck and drew her to him. His lips captured hers in a hard kiss. Her arms curled around his waist, and her tongue traced his lips.

Colby groaned as he broke the kiss. "Later, sweetheart." He released her and turned to do his job. But it wasn't going to be easy, not with her waiting for him.

* * * *

"How are you still standing?" Sierra asked.

"I don't know." Lara sank down onto the sofa. That

kiss. Oh, that kiss. It was one of passion and possession. Anyone seeing it would know she belonged to Colby. Did she? Her lips tilted up. Yes, she did belong to him, at least for now.

"I'm glad Colby found someone like you," said Tessa.

"What do you mean?"

"That came out the wrong way. You're perfect for him, Lara. The two of you together, I don't know. You just fit."

Lara relaxed. "Thank you, Tessa. Tell me more about this book club."

The book club was what she thought, reading hot romances. It sounded fabulous, and Lara couldn't wait.

A little while later, Lara stood up and stretched. While her clothing was comfortable, she needed to stretch every now and then. A man approached the back of the sofa.

A tall man with serious brown eyes and short-cropped black hair stood there, smiling at the women. "Good evening ladies. And who is this new one?"

"Good evening," Lara said. Good manners dictated she at least acknowledge him.

"Are you willing to play with me?" His voice was soft and slid over her skin like a silky caress.

Wow. Talk about a smooth talker. Lara pasted a smile on her face and held up her wrist. "I'm taken."

"I'm sure he won't mind if I borrow you for little while."

What the heck was going on here? She didn't expect to get hit on here with her wrist band and all the rules, let alone that her Dom was a monitor. Meanwhile, Sierra and Tessa were giggling. What was that about? "I would mind." Lara stared him down. He looked familiar, but she couldn't quite place him. "I'm sure there are some very lovely, unattached, women here for you."

"You wound me, dear lady." He placed his hand over his heart. "I only want to play with you."

Lara couldn't help it, her lips twitched. "Again, I'm taken, and I don't cheat."

This time, Sierra and Tessa burst out laughing. "Give it up, Zeke." Sierra said.

"Zeke?" His name was familiar. "Wait a second. Don't you own Riggs Construction?"

"At your service." He gave her a little bow, which caused Sierra and Tessa to start laughing again.

"You can stop with the flirting; it doesn't work on me." Actually, it might have, if she wasn't with Colby. But that was neither here nor there; she was faithful to the man she had a relationship with.

"You just had to try, didn't you?" Colby asked as he walked up to Lara and put his arm around her waist.

"What better way to test a woman's loyalties," Zeke said. "I'm happy to say she passed with flying colors."

Lara glared at Zeke. "You were testing me?"

Zeke held his hands up in front of him. "Sorry, just had to make sure you were the right woman for my man Colby here."

"Zeke, go find Melanie. She was looking for you earlier," Colby said. "Don't forget your shift starts in two hours."

"I won't, and off I go to have some fun." Zeke moved away, and Lara looked up at Colby.

"What was that all about?" Lara asked.

"Zeke just being Zeke." They'd become good friends when he'd done some work in the shop for Colby, and now they worked together at the club. "And before you ask, no, I didn't send him over. I trust you."

"You better." She glanced around the club, amazed at

how busy it had gotten over the last few hours. "Are you off shift now?"

"Yes. Are you ready to take a stroll?"

"I am." Lara looked over at Sierra and Tessa.

"Oh, don't mind us. Our men are on their way over," Tessa said with a flirty grin.

"Let's go." With his arm around her waist, Colby led Lara from the green area and out into the club.

Then the music hit her. A wild beat that resonated deep within her body. Colby leaned down. "Shall we start with the bondage scene?"

The music wasn't so loud she couldn't hear him. Interesting. At the other kink gatherings she'd attended, the music had been super loud, and she could hardly hear anyone talk. "That sounds perfect."

Colby guided her to the bondage scene that was just being set up. "How do you want to do this?"

"What do you mean, Sir?" Damn, earlier she'd forgotten the Sir. Had Colby noticed? Would he punish her? And why did that thought make her hot?

"We can stand, or we can sit." He tilted her head up until their gazes met. "And by sitting, I mean you will either be on my lap or sitting between my legs."

Lara tilted her head. Colby hadn't mentioned anything like that before. How did she feel about it? Sitting in his lap felt a little too intimate. They hadn't had more than kisses the last couple of weeks.

"Can you explain what you mean about me sitting between your legs, Sir?"

"It's easier to show you, especially if sitting in my lap is out of the question." He led her to the sofa sitting in front of the stage. He grabbed one of the oversized pillows and placed it on the floor.

She realized what he was doing. "I get it now, Sir."

"Good. Let me help you onto the pillow."

Lara did as Colby asked. And he slowly lowered her until her butt rested fully on the pillow. Colby straightened and smiled. She tilted her head back and stared up at him. "But where are you sitting, Sir?"

"Behind you." Colby maneuvered around her. "Lean right just for a moment." Lara did as he said, and Colby sat down with both legs next to her left shoulder. "All right, now close your eyes, lean left, and duck your head."

She took a deep breath and followed his directions. Colby's body shifted behind her and then… His legs were on either side of her. She opened her eyes. Yep. He was now straddling her back. "Wouldn't it have been easier if you sat down first, Sir?"

"Maybe." Colby shifted once again, the heat from his body encompassing hers. "Rest back against the sofa," he said, his palms on her shoulders.

Lara took a deep breath and let it out, forcing herself to relax. Colby's legs pressed up against her arms, and Lara laid her hands in her lap. Colby shifted behind her again, and his crotch was pressed closer to her back. She fought not to squirm as the ridge of his cock made itself known.

"Now as we watch the scene, I'll be able to touch you."

As if to prove his point, he lightly traced her collarbone, following the line of the leather halter-top until he came to her breast. Then he splayed his fingers over her breast.

Her breath caught in her throat at the feel of his hand cupping her breast even with the fabric between them. She hadn't expected this strong sensation. Not this intense need.

"Remember," he said softly, his breath brushing her ear. "I've read your questionnaire. We'll take it slow. And

I'll warn you when I want to untie your top so I can touch your luscious globes."

She didn't think her body could get any hotter, but it did. Especially when Colby's fingers played with the laces down the front of the halter top.

"Now pay attention, sweetheart. The scene is about to begin."

Lara focused on the stage. A sub stood off to the side as the Dom arranged everything on the table to his satisfaction.

"Tonight, you get to see David, who is one of the long-time Doms in the club, and Regina, one of the long-time subs. Regina is a club sub."

"Is Dom David in a committed relationship, Sir?"

"Yes, he is. David is married. His wife understands about his wanting to be in a club. She doesn't mind playing at home; she just won't do it in the club. So David will play with one of the club subs when they request it."

"And Regina, Sir?"

"Regina is unattached. She's played with David before, and they enjoy playing together. And no, they don't have sex."

She blew out a breath. His reminder made her feel better. She wasn't sure how she would feel if someone was cheating on their spouse and she was watching. What was she thinking? It could be a polyamorous arrangement, which was perfectly fine.

"How long have you been a monitor here at the club, Sir?"

"A couple of months. Zeke and I were asked if we would do it. We have both been part of the club since right after it opened."

"So that means…" She tilted her head back. "You've

played with some of the club subs, Sir?"

"Yes, my sweet." His fingers traced her neck and she shivered. "But I didn't have sex with them."

Lara let out a breath. "Am I questioning too much, Sir?"

"No. There has to be honesty between us, and I'd rather you ask questions than for there to be any misunderstandings."

"Thank you, Sir." Lara lowered her head and returned her attention to the stage. Regina had removed her clothing. For just a moment, Lara was shocked, but then she realized there was nothing to be shocked about. They were all consenting adults.

David held out what looked like a pair of roped panties. He helped Regina into them before he led Regina over to an unusual looking chair. Lara hadn't seen a chair like that before. It was made of wood and had a bar across the top that one could use to secure a sub's arms.

The bottom half of the chair was different. The seat was split, and Lara couldn't figure out why.

"I know we have some new people here tonight," David's voice rang clear through the area. "Regina enjoys being bound, so tonight, I'm going to use the bondage chair and show you some different ways you can tie up your sub."

Lara shifted on the pillow and kept her gaze on the couple on stage. The Dom picked up several strands of rope.

"For the newer people out there, I'm using hemp rope today. Hemp rope is good because it's strong yet soft. If you're new to bondage, this is an expensive rope." As David talked, he began to tie Regina's left arm. The purple rope stood out against her creamy skin and the dark wood of the chair.

"I like using hemp because it allows me to use fewer knots. You'll also see hemp used with Shibari."

"Have you ever seen Shibari?" Colby asked her.

"No, Sir." Lara kept her gaze on the couple, fascinated by the way David moved around Regina as he secured her arms into place. How would it feel if Colby did that to her? Her pussy muscles tightened, and her breasts swelled.

"I'll make sure you see a demonstration. Shibari can be very sensual."

He lightly ran his fingers up and down her arms, his rough skin against her soft skin creating a delicious sensation.

"Now, I'm sure some of you are wondering why I selected this chair in particular." David knelt behind the chair and reached underneath, then he stood up. "This chair has a very special feature."

He moved around and stood off to the left-hand side, then reached over and put his hand on the inside of Regina's thigh and pressed outward.

Lara's breath caught in her throat as Regina's legs started to part. "So that's what the split is for," she whispered.

"It's ingenious," Colby whispered, his breath brushing her skin. "David released the pin that holds the legs closed. Now he can position her anyway he likes."

A tremor went through Lara's body. She kept her gaze on the couple. Within just a few minutes, Regina's legs were tied to the chair. Lara squirmed on the pillow.

"Your skin is flushed. Is that from my touch or from what you're seeing?" Colby asked.

"Both, Sir." It was from both. Maybe a little bit more from his touch than what she was seeing. But both were arousing. As was the way he paid so much attention to her reactions.

"I'll have to see what I can do about that." His fingers moved to the laces in the front of the halter. "I'm going to unlace your top now."

Her mouth went dry. She nodded and waited.

"Words, sweetheart."

Swallowing, Lara wet her lips. "Yes, I understand, Sir. You're going to undo my top." Her heart sped up. *Trust him.*

Colby released the bow at the bottom of the leather and gently loosened the fabric.

Lara could barely breathe as he loosened the top. Colby was careful as he removed the laces from the front. When he had the tie in his hand, he carefully rolled it up and teased the skin between her breasts with it.

"Hold on to this for me, sweetheart." He put the tie in her hand, and Lara closed her fingers around it.

While the top was loose, it still covered her breasts. She almost let out a sigh of relief, then Colby's hands slipped between the fabric and her skin. She couldn't help the small moan that left her lips as he cupped her breasts.

"So soft, perfect for my hands," he whispered.

She squirmed with heat and desire.

He adjusted his hands, and his thumbs brushed over her nipples. They hardened into tight peaks.

"Is that for me?" There was laughter in his voice.

Lara's lashes fell.

"Oh no, my sweet." He pinched her right nipple. "Keep those eyes open and watch what is happening in the scene."

Lara forced her eyes open to see that David was using the ropes on Regina's breasts. A quiver went up her spine. "That has to hurt, Sir."

David had the ropes above and below Regina's breast, constricting them between the ropes.

"Look at her face; does she look like she's in pain?"

Lara forced her gaze to Regina's face. Regina's lips were parted, and her breathing was a little choppy. But her eyes were alight with excitement and maybe pleasure.

"No, Sir. She looks like she's enjoying it."

"Very good. Regina enjoys being bound, no matter how it's done. But keep watching because David is not through with her yet."

Lara tried to control her breathing as she continued to watch David bind Regina. When he was done, he'd created a very interesting work of art. What Lara didn't understand was why he'd made Regina wear what looked like a rope bikini around her crotch.

David stroked Regina's skin and spoke softly to her. Lara couldn't hear the words, but she saw Regina's lips moving and the slight smile that curved her lips.

"Sir?" Lara said.

"What is it, my sweet?" His fingers toyed with her nipples, keeping them hard and wanting. Wanting more.

"Why do I feel like David is up to something, Sir?"

"Very perceptive you are." He kissed her cheek. "Just keep watching. Plus, have you noticed how David touches Regina. She has a safe word, and if he goes too far, she'll say it, and he'll stop."

"I remember the discussion about safe words, Sir." She'd never heard anyone use one. Even when she thought they should.

"Keep your gaze on Regina. See how her body is flushed. That's one sign David is on the right track. Her breathing would be another. But there are other subtle hints. The way her fingers curl into her palms and then release.

The slight shifting of her body in the chair and whether her eyes widen or narrow."

Lara's gaze took in each of those places as Colby talked. Yes, he was right. "Is it always like that, Sir?"

"Depends on the sub. For example…" He pinched her left nipple, and she jumped. "You jumped, but tell me: What else are you feeling?"

"Heat and a zing. It's the best way I can describe it, from my nipple to my clit, Sir."

"I felt you jump, but what I see is the flushing of your skin and you biting into your lower lip as if you were stopping yourself from crying out."

Lara leaned her head back and gazed up at Colby. "I did, Sir?"

"Yes and I can understand why you did it here in the club. But when we're alone, I want to hear everything."

A squeal from the stage captured Lara attention. Regina was squirming in the chair with David standing next to it, a wide grin plastered on his face.

"I believe I missed something, Sir."

"You did, sweetheart." Colby's fingers slid down to Lara's abdomen. "Earlier when you asked if David was up to something, you were correct. You see, he's placed a vibrating bullet inside the rope bikini he made for Regina."

His fingers toyed with the top of her leather skirt.

Lara kept her gaze on Regina, trying not to squirm beneath Colby's touch. When Colby's finger slipped beneath the waistband of the skirt, Lara tensed. "Ummmm, Sir. Ah, yellow, Sir."

Colby's fingers stilled. "What is it, sweetheart? Am I moving too fast?"

"Yes… No… I don't think I'm ready for that level of play in public yet, Sir." Her body protested at her words, but she wasn't ready for this level of play. She was barely tolerating the exposure of her breasts.

"I understand." His fingers moved back to her abdomen. "I want you to do something."

"What is that, Sir?"

"I want you to look down and tell me what you see."

Lara's breath caught in her throat. She could do this. She tilted her head down. Her breath whooshed out of her. Even though Colby had untied the front of the halter top it still covered her breasts; nothing was really exposed except the skin between her breasts.

"I… You made sure I was covered even though you were playing with my breasts, Sir."

"Correct. This is your first full night, and I want you to feel comfortable. I'm aware that exposing you on the first night would not be a good idea. Trust goes both ways."

He was right. "I trust you, Sir." She did, or she wouldn't be in the club with him, but doing this was deepening that trust.

"Sir! I need to come, Sir," Regina yelled, pulling Lara's attention back to the stage.

Regina's head was moving from side to side, her fingers curled into her hands and her legs were shaking.

"Please, Sir," Regina said.

David put his hand on Regina's head. "Come for me. You have my permission."

Regina let out a cry.

"Is it standard protocol, Sir, for a sub to ask for permission to orgasm?" Lara was confused. She didn't remember reading about that. She remembered club protocol about how to address Doms and subs, but nothing about this.

"Depends on the couple. David likes his subs to ask for

permission, and Regina is well aware of it."

"Will you make me ask for permission, Sir?" Lara tilted her head so she could see Colby's face.

"Maybe, but only when I want to push your boundaries. For me, pleasure is the name of the game. Your pleasure gives me pleasure." Colby's arms tightened around her. "Now, look back at the stage and tell me what you see."

Lara's gaze returned to the stage, and her heart jumped a beat. "Regina's head is bent, and David is quietly speaking to her while he's undoing the ropes on her arms. He's rubbing her arms as he talks. Regina looks…like she's, I don't know quite the word, like maybe her thoughts are far away from where she is."

"Very close. She's on the edge of subspace."

"I've read about that."

"Some subs reach it very easily, and for others, it takes more time. Others never reach it."

Lara continued to watch as David untied Regina. When he was done, he grabbed the blanket, wrapped it around her, and carried her off the stage to a sofa. David said something to Jordan, who nodded. David then went back on the stage and began cleaning up.

"Bend forward again, sweetheart."

Lara did as he asked, and Colby swung his leg over her, then stood up and stretched.

Her mouth watered as his t-shirt molded to his chest and arms. The man was built. Not overly muscular, but enough he could stop women in their tracks. Her included.

"Let me help you up." Lara bent her knees and put her hands in Colby's. He pulled her up. Lara stumbled into Colby, and he steadied her.

"Easy." He held her close until her legs could hold her

up. "Let's go sit over in the quiet area and talk." Colby took her hand and led her over past Regina, who was now being held by David, to an overstuffed set of chairs.

Once they got to the chairs, Colby sat down while still holding onto her hand. "Would you please sit on my lap?"

His soft question caused Lara to pause. Then, without questioning herself, she nodded and allowed Colby to pull her down until she was seated on his lap. His wide smile made her body tingle with pleasure.

"So how did you like watching that scene?" Colby asked.

Lara thought for a moment. "It was different than I thought, but also very nice." She shrugged. "I don't know how to explain it."

"It will get easier, but first things first. Protocol in the club with your Dom."

"Oh, crap. Sorry, Sir." She needed to remember to tack on the sir. She hadn't had a Dom so fully into the lifestyle before.

"I'm not going to punish you tonight for forgetting, but this is your only warning."

"Yes, Sir." She wouldn't forget.

"I'd like to discuss our next time here at the club. Would you prefer Saturday nights?"

"I would. The café is closed on Sundays so that really helps if I have a late night, Sir."

"I can do that. I'm going to suggest next Thursday night we come and play. We can make it an early night, I'll have you home by eleven."

"Why Thursday night, Sir?"

"The club is less crowded, and I'd love to see you topless in the club. Thursday would be a good night for you to try without feeling pressured."

Lara swallowed. "I can try, Sir."

"I'm pushing your comfort zone a little bit. Tonight, when you were watching Regina on stage. At any point did you focus on her nudity?"

Lara shook her head. "Maybe when she first sat down, but after that, no, Sir."

"Does it help you know that many won't even notice you're topless?"

Lara swallowed. "Can I think about it, Sir?"

"Yes." He traced her cheek. "Does it bother you?"

She nodded. "I..." Her eyes closed. "I guess I'm thinking about my business. Every time I see someone, I'll be thinking about being topless here and if they've seen me, Sir." All she could hear was her mother's voice when she was younger, telling her appearance was everything.

Colby tucked her close to him. "I understand."

"Is that going to affect our relationship, Sir?"

"No." His voice was firm.

"Are you sure, Sir?"

"Are you questioning your Dom, sweetheart?" His voice dropped an octave.

"No, Sir." She wasn't questioning him, not really. Lara wanted to nip the issue in the bud before she got in too deep. If Colby had a problem with her staying dressed in the club, then she wanted it addressed.

"I can hear you thinking." Colby shifted. "Are you ready to go home?"

"Yes, Sir."

Colby helped her to her feet and had her stand in front of him while he laced the halter top back together. She'd forgotten he'd undone it. Lara would have to think about that.

He took her hand and walked her to the ladies' room.

She slipped inside and got her things out of the locker, put her coat on, and came back out. He was standing there, a small bag in his hand.

The ride to her home was quiet. When he pulled up in front of her duplex, Colby reached over, put his fingers on her chin, and she turned her head.

"I heard you thinking all the way here. There is no right or wrong, Lara. The relationship is what we make it."

"But what if I can't play in the club?" She was having serious doubts. Doubts because of her family ties.

"We'll play at home in private until you're more comfortable."

"But—"

He put his fingers over her lips. "Let's not borrow trouble. Now give me your phone."

Lara fumbled in her purse, held her finger on the sensor, then handed the phone to him. "You already have my cell number, but I see you didn't put it in your phone." He gave her the phone back and climbed out of the car.

Colby walked her up the steps and waited until she unlocked the door and turned the alarm off. "Any questions or concerns, and I mean anything that comes up, call me. I'll see you Monday." He brushed his lips over hers and waited until she stepped inside and closed the door. "And no getting yourself off, sweetheart. That's my job."

Lara's forehead hit the wood of the doorframe. How did he know? That man saw things she wasn't sure she wanted him to see. She locked up, set the alarm, and made her way into her bedroom. She had a lot to think about.

* * * *

Colby sat in the borrowed car and stared at Lara's place. He didn't want to leave her, but he needed to let her work through tonight. He only hoped she'd call him or

Sierra, or one of the other women she was friends with if she needed to talk. That reminded him, Max mentioned about starting a sub group where they could talk freely within their group. He'd have to check to see where they were on that and ask Lara to join.

While she might have had *some* experience in college, it wasn't anything like the club. And he suspected Lara hadn't played much. She had knowledge, but not practical experience. That wasn't odd; it happened. He started the engine and drove home. He'd return the car to Damon tomorrow and get his bike.

Once inside his apartment, Colby undressed and put the clothes in the hamper before he stepped into the shower. He'd give Lara Sunday to think about tonight, then go to the café on Monday to chat. It wouldn't be the conversation he wanted, but he'd be able to tell if she was pulling away.

He'd give her some time to process and cook her dinner on Tuesday night, and they could have a nice private chat. He meant what he said tonight: if she couldn't play in the club, they'd play into the bedroom until she could.

The relationship was new, and it would take time to figure out. In the meantime, he already had more ideas about clothing. Tomorrow, he'd go into his workshop and start working on them.

* * * *

Colby walked into Lara's café Monday morning to see her all but dancing to the music she had on. There were two couples in the café having breakfast. It was early yet, barely nine. He walked up to the counter.

"Good morning, beautiful."

Lara spun around and grinned. "Good morning, Colby."

"I'm going to snag a table over in the corner."

"No problem. It's quiet right now. Your usual?"

"Surprise me." Her eyes widened. "Just not too crazy, please."

"Hmmm." Mischief danced across her features, and she laughed. "I promise." She leaned in closer. "Sir," she whispered before twirling away.

His cock twitched, and he almost reached out to haul her into his arms but fought the urge. This was her place of business. Colby went over to the table of four and pulled out his sketchpad.

Within a few minutes, Lara came over with coffee and food. "Nothing too dangerous. Coffee with a hint of nutmeg and a breakfast sandwich." She set everything down and walked away to help another couple.

Colby took a sip of his coffee. The nutmeg gave the drink a little bit of a kick. He picked up the breakfast sandwich and grinned. Ham, bacon, sausage, and cheese—lots of it.

While he ate, he opened his sketchbook and adjusted some of the drawings of floggers.

"Now that looks nice," a male voice said.

Colby looked up. "Hi, guys, sit down, and I'll show you what I've designed." Bear and Flash, regulars at the shop, sat down. Lara came bustling over.

"You guys need anything?" she asked.

"You don't have to serve us," Bear said.

"True, but it's quiet right now, and I don't mind."

Bear smiled. "Black coffee and two of whatever Colby is eating."

"Hot tea, breakfast blend, and your egg white and spinach wrap." Flash gave his order.

"Coming right up."

The men watched her walk away. "Nice butt," Flash

commented.

"Back off." Colby's voice deepened. "She's off limits."

Bear's eyebrows rose. "So that's how it is."

Colby stared at Bear. His name fit him. He was a big guy, built like a bear. And Flash, yeah, his name fit too due to the bright colors of his shirts. "Yes. So you want to see the designs?" Colby tried to get his temper under control. Bear didn't mean anything by his words, but still, Colby bristled.

"Yeah, let's see what you came up with," Bear said.

Colby pushed the sketch book over to them. "There are four different designs." He kept an eye on Lara as she prepared food and drinks for the guys. When she picked up a tray with everything, he started to push back his chair, but she glared at him.

Okay. Her job. And she knew what she was doing. Once at the table, she balanced the tray on the table and set out the food.

"Thank you," Flash said with a smile.

"Smells delicious." Bear picked up his first breakfast sandwich and took a big bite.

Lara's eyes widened as almost half of the sandwich disappeared. Colby chuckled. "The name Bear fits," he told Lara.

"So I see." She turned and went back behind the counter.

"These are nice," Bear said, pointing to the sketches.

"Yes, but I like the handle on this one." Flash pointed to the first sketch. "And the tails on this one." He turned to the fourth sketch.

"I can work with that." Colby rubbed his chin.

"Great. That's the one I want." Flash took a bite of his wrap.

"I like the second one the best." Bear flipped the pages after wiping his hands off. "The design is very nice."

"Thank you. How soon do you need them?"

"Two weeks, can you do that?" Bear asked.

"Shouldn't be a problem. Thuddy or stingy?"

Bear took a drink of his coffee.

"Thuddy for me," Flash said. "The heavier the better."

Colby nodded and made a note on his sketch pad.

"I'd like mine with fewer tails, about medium heaviness," Bear said.

"So closer to a sting than a thud?" Colby asked.

"Yeah." A smile crossed Bear's face as a shadow fell over the table.

"More coffee or hot water?" Lara asked, standing there.

"Please," Bear said holding his cup out.

Lara refilled Bear's cup and then his.

"I'm good," Flash said.

"Enjoy."

"Now I know why you wanted to meet here," Bear said.

"Oh?" Hadn't his warning come across?

"Great food." Flash grinned.

Colby shook his head as they finished their conversation and drinks. All three stood and shook hands. Bear and Flash picked up their trash and carried it over to the bin, then walked over to the counter.

Lara smiled at them as they paid, then Bear put money in the tip jar and left with a wave at Colby.

He cleaned up his stuff and picked up his sketchbook. When he approached Lara, she was frowning at the tip jar.

"What is it?" he asked. It didn't make sense why she would be frowning at the tip jar.

"Colby, they left a twenty dollar tip." Her voice was

soft.

"Yes."

"It's way too much." She shook her head.

"Honey," he said softly. "It's because they appreciate how you treat them."

"But..." Her cheeks turned red.

"You don't ignore them or ask them to leave your café."

"Why would I?"

"They're bikers."

"They're people. It doesn't matter if they're bikers or businessmen or students."

"And that's why they left you a big tip."

Lara sighed, emptied the tip jar and put it back. "So you sketch?" She pointed to the book in his hand.

"It's the best when someone wants a custom piece."

"Will you show me your sketches?"

"Dinner tomorrow night and I'll show you all my sketches."

"Including the naughty ones?" Her eyes twinkled with mischief.

"They're all naughty." He leaned over and brushed a kiss over her lips, then left the café before he decided on more than just a chaste kiss.

* * * *

Lara grinned as she watched Colby leave the café. His brief kiss sent tingles through her body.

Two-thirty in the afternoon arrived faster than Lara expected. The café had been filled with a steady stream of customers. A half an hour before closing, she started cleaning up the café. She'd already sent Eve home.

When the door opened, she turned and saw her brother. "Damn," she whispered under her breath. "I'm getting ready to close up, Keith."

"This will only take a minute." He stood in front of the door.

Lara sighed. "Fine. What do you want?" There would never be warm fuzzy feelings between her and her family.

"To talk."

"We have nothing to talk about." Wasn't that the truth?

"We do, and you will listen." He crossed his arms over his chest.

Lara ignored him and continued to clean up.

"I want you to know that we're watching you, and you need to walk the straight and narrow."

"What?" She whirled around and glared at her brother. What the hell did he mean by that? Why the hell did she care? "Get out." She'd had enough of her family.

"Stay calm. I wanted you to know so you can clean up your act. Father isn't happy."

"I don't care. This is my life and my business. I'm tired of my *family* trying to decide what is best for me." She marched over to him and pushed the door open. "Get out, and don't come back. And tell Father, if he keeps this crap up, he'll never see me again." She shoved him out the door and locked it once he was outside.

"We're watching," Keith said once again before walking away.

Lara sagged against the door. What the hell was that about? Her family was watching her? Unease settled in the pit of her stomach, but she pushed it away as she finished cleaning up and closing down the café for the day.

Her family could go to hell as far as she was concerned. She wasn't so much worried about herself, but what about Colby, or the club and her new friends there. Damn it. Leaving the café, she set the alarm and locked the back door.

Out of habit, she looked around before moving to her car, but after she got in and locked the doors, she glanced in her rear-view mirror. Nothing. *Paranoid, are we?*

Lara blew out a breath and started her car and drove home. Aunt Tammy was sitting outside when Lara pulled up.

"Everything okay, Aunt Tammy?" she asked as she climbed out of her vehicle.

"Fine. Just getting some sun."

She breathed a sigh of relief. While her family usually didn't bother Aunt Tammy, she wouldn't put it past them. "That's nice. Want some tea?"

"I would love some." Aunt Tammy walked up the steps with her into Lara's duplex. "So tell me: What has you rattled?" her aunt asked after Lara had tea and cookies on the table.

"Nothing," Lara answered automatically.

"Young lady." Aunt Tammy stared at her. "I know when you're upset."

Lara sat down and gave her aunt a sad smile. "I never could hide anything from you."

"And don't you forget it. Out with it."

"Keith stopped by the café as I was closing down today."

"What did that no good nephew of mine want?"

Lara took a sip of her tea. "He said they were watching me."

Aunt Tammy laughed. "Let them watch."

"But." How much should she tell her aunt? She wouldn't tell her about the club. "Why would they watch me?" An icy shiver slid up her spine. With her dating Colby and them going to the club, there were more people involved than just her and her aunt.

"Because they're control freaks. Lara, honey,"—her aunt patted her on the arm—"don't let them get to you. So when is the next date with your young man, Colby?"

"Tomorrow."

Colby. If her family was watching, they already knew about him, but how much, she didn't know. She'd have to ask Colby about security at the club. It seemed pretty tight to her, but her family was worse than bloodhounds at times. "We're having dinner."

"Good." Aunt Tammy sipped her tea. "Don't let Keith get to you. He's trying to rattle you and make you doubt yourself."

He's not doing a bad job, Lara said to herself. She didn't want to worry her aunt. "You're right. So who's cooking tonight?"

"I say we call for pizza and enjoy ourselves with a movie. I'm dying to watch that one about the guys that strip for a living."

Lara laughed. "Pizza and a movie it is."

Chapter 8

Lara pushed her food around on her plate. Colby had brought her to his apartment for dinner, but she didn't have much of an appetite. Not after she saw some man taking pictures across the street from her café. He could have been a tourist, but something about him bothered her.

"What's wrong, honey?" Colby asked.

"What?" Lara shook her head. "Nothing. I'm not hungry." Spaghetti, meatballs, and garlic bread were her favorites, but tonight the meal sat like a lead ball in her stomach.

Colby stood with his empty plate, and Lara started to stand. "I'll take care of it." While his tone wasn't angry, it was hard and deep. "Why don't you go sit on the sofa?" His voice was softer this time.

"Are you sure I can't help?"

"Go."

Lara made her way over to his leather sofa and sat down. The buttery soft leather cradled her body. Colby explained he lived above the garage to be close to his mother if she needed help.

She smiled. He was a good man. And just like a man, he had a huge TV. She could picture Colby sitting here with his feet up on the table, beer in hand, watching some sporting event or car race.

The next thing she knew, Colby plucked her from her

seat and had her in his lap. Not that she minded, she liked being in his arms.

"Time to spill," he said, one arm around her waist and his free hand cupping her face and turning her to face him.

"Spill what?" Damn, was she an open book with everyone? First her aunt and now Colby.

Colby gave her that hard, Dom look she wondered if Max had taught him. She let out a sigh. "It's nothing." Why was she going to confess anything to him?

He tilted her chin up and stared at her. Lara squirmed. "Do they teach you that look in Dom school or something?"

Colby leaned his head back and let out a roar of laughter before looking at her again. "Why, yes, they do. Talk."

Lara squirmed in his lap. "I'm just being silly."

"Something has you upset, so let me be the judge if you're silly or not."

"Why does it matter so much?" The more she thought about it, the more she thought she'd imagined the guy taking pictures today.

"Are we in a relationship?" he asked.

"I'd like to think so."

"Part of a relationship is talking to the other person, especially when something is bothering them. I can't fix it if I don't know about it."

"Why would you want to fix it?" She tilted her head.

"Because I'm a man."

Lara let out a laugh. "Such a guy thing."

"You bet. Now tell me."

"I'm blowing this out of proportion; I know I am. Keith stopped by the café yesterday afternoon, right before I closed."

"What did he want?"

"To make a nuisance out of himself."

"It was more than that, or you wouldn't be upset."

Lara wrinkled her nose. "He told me I was being watched."

Colby stiffened. "By who?"

A tremor slid up her spine at his quiet words. "Colby, you can't confront him." She could see the headlines her father would make sure happened. *Local Leather Shop Owner Attacks Banker's Son.*

"He threatened you." Colby's voice was hard and cold.

"My family is always threatening me." The minute the words left her lips, she froze. Colby stiffened even as his arms tightened around her. "That came out wrong."

"I don't think so." Fingers nudged her chin up. "What have they done before?"

Lara sighed. "I'm considered the black sheep of my family. I told you how they've reacted to things I've done in the past."

"Yes, but you never mentioned any threats."

"It's just little things, like my mom calling me over for dinner and pushing Walter at me even though we're divorced, and I've told her we're not getting back together. Or my dad, who was angry I insisted on certain protections in my business loan from his bank." Yeah, that hadn't been a fun conversation. "You saw how Keith and Walter were with the bikers. It's stuff like that."

"They're making your life hell," Colby whispered.

"They try." Having Colby's arms around her made her feel safe. "I think this was just Keith trying to rattle me, and it worked."

"It was more than his words, wasn't it?"

"I thought I saw someone taking pictures across the street from the café today."

Colby's eyes narrowed.

"I'm sure it was just some tourist."

"Yet it bothered you." Colby lowered his head. "If anything happens, and I mean anything, even if it's just a feeling, you call me, or better yet, if any of the bikers are in the café, tell them. I'll spread the word."

Lara shook her head. "I don't want anyone to get into trouble."

"No one will. I don't like this, Lara. Your family is abusive."

She considered his words. "Dysfunctional."

"Semantics. I want you to promise me, if anything happens, you'll call me. Even the slightest thing."

Lara stared at him. "I can only promise to call you after the event, during the event may be too difficult." Especially if she had to get the police involved. "Weren't you going to show me your sketches?" she said, trying to get their conversation off her and her crazy family.

"I'm not forgetting this." He slid her from his lap onto the sofa. "I'll get my sketchbook because I did promise you, and I don't go back on my word. Remember that, Lara. Because I give you my word: I will keep you safe."

Warmth filled Lara's veins at Colby's words. She believed he would keep her safe, even if meant him getting into trouble. Well, she wasn't going to allow that to happen. She would protect him as he protected her. He didn't realize how vicious her family could be.

* * * *

Lara stood staring at her closet on Thursday evening. What to wear tonight? She had a skirt already picked out, but the top was the issue. She wanted something easy on and easy off.

A shiver slid over her skin. Tonight, she was going to

try and go topless at the club. Not that she thought it was a bad idea, but she was still nervous about it. She finally settled on a lacy blouse she'd bought years ago, but thought was too sheer to wear outside the house.

She dressed and applied her makeup before glancing at the clock. Colby would be here any minute. Lara slipped on a pair of ballet slippers and a jacket. Barely a minute later, her doorbell rang.

"Hi."

"Hello, beautiful." Colby leaned down and gave her a kiss. "Ready?"

"Yes." Lara grabbed her purse. "Whose car do you keep borrowing?" she asked as he led her down the steps.

"Damon's. It's a little hard to ask you to ride my bike when you're already dressed for the club."

"How about this next time. Ride your bike here and we take my car?"

"Are you sure?"

"Yes." He was always so concerned about her. "It's silly for you to keep borrowing a car." Besides, if her family was watching, it would freak them out to see his motorcycle parked outside her home late at night. She smiled at the thought of making her family crazy.

"So, this weekend you're catering at the club again?" Colby asked as he drove.

"Yes, Max wants to do it once a month and see how it goes."

"Shall I come by the café and help you?"

"If you like. Pretty much everything will be ready. I'll just need to load the hot boxes and other stuff."

"If Max is going to continue having you bring food, you need to talk with him about keeping some supplies at the club so you don't have to bring so much."

"That's not a bad idea." Lara shifted in her seat.

"Nervous about tonight?"

"A little."

"You don't have to go topless; it's all up to you." Colby reached over and took her hand.

"I know, but I'd like to try." She forced her mother's nagging words that appearances were everything to the back of her mind. This was for her and Colby.

Colby turned down the driveway and stopped at the gate. After punching in a code, the gate opened, and Colby drove through. They parked and made their way into the club. "Go put your things away; I'll be in the club waiting for you."

"Yes, Sir."

Once inside the ladies' bathroom, Lara took a deep breath. Okay, she could do this. She put her jacket and purse inside a locker and shut it. Lara checked her hair and makeup before leaving the room.

Colby was just inside the club doors when she walked in. The second the music reached her ears, her body settled. The music had a primal beat to it.

His gaze went from her head to her toes, to come back and linger at her top. "Nice top."

Her face flushed. "I hope you approve, Sir." She began to lift her arms then dropped them back to her sides. This was going to be hard for her.

Colby's lips twitched, and she glared at him, then realized he was only wearing a pair of pants, no shoes and no shirt. "Won't you get cold, Sir?"

"With you in the room, the temperature is always hot." He captured her wrist before she could curve her arm over her chest as another Dom walked by with a glance at her.

"Lara." His warm fingers cupped her chin and lifted

her face. "I can't stop anyone from looking at my beautiful partner, but I can promise you no one else will touch you."

Air rushed out of Lara's lungs. She hadn't even realized she was afraid of someone else touching her until Colby said it. "Thank you, Sir."

"You're mine, sweetheart. No one else's." He brushed a kiss over her forehead, then looked around the room. "There's a flogging scene going on; would you like to go watch?"

"Yes, Sir." Maybe if she focused her attention elsewhere, she'd forget how exposed she was in this lacy top. Colby led her over to the scene and found a place for them to sit. Or should she say he sat and pulled her into his lap. Her back was against his chest, and his arms rested around her waist.

Lara kept her concentration on the couple on stage instead of Colby's arms around her or the heat coming from his body, seeping into her skin. The sub on the stage was tied to a St. Andrew's Cross, nude. The Dom had on pants and loafers. What was it about these men going shirtless?

"See the flogger in his hand?" Colby whispered. She nodded. "That one has more tails—or falls—to it. It will create a thuddy feeling. It's a good one to warm up with."

The Dom brought his arm back and let it fly. Lara flinched when the flogger made contact with the sub's ass.

"That's got to hurt, Sir."

Colby tapped his fingers against her arm, not hard, but the impact was there. "Did that hurt?"

"No, Sir."

"That's what the sub is feeling. Both are experienced with flogging."

"But..." Lara shook her head. "I'm sorry, Sir; I just don't get it."

"Think of it this way, how did my fingers feel against your skin were when I tapped you?"

"Soft and gentle, Sir."

"Now think about how it feels when someone pinches you or snaps a towel that hits your butt. What's the difference?"

"Oh." She tilted her head. "So what you did with your fingers is considered thuddy, but a snap of towel would be stingee, Sir."

"Simplified, but yes. The heavier the flogger is and the wider the tails or the number of tails, the more thuddy it will be. Some subs like both, some only thuddy, some only stingee."

"Why do I have a feeling stingee, even though you said like a snap of a towel, is so much more than that, Sir?"

"It can be. It all depends."

Lara considered his words. "It sounds like you've tried it, Sir."

"I have." He leaned closer to her. "Most Doms have. I'm not going to say all, because I don't know all the Doms at the club personally, but I do know many of us wouldn't do something to a sub we haven't already tried."

"Who would dare flog a Dom, Sir?"

"You'd be surprised."

What he said made sense, but still, who would want to take on a man like Colby, let alone someone like Max? She shifted on Colby's lap. The Dom switched floggers, and Lara kept her gaze on the scene.

The sub would moan every so often, but Lara noticed the Dom didn't strike in the same place, but moved around, then came back to that first place. He also paused and rubbed the areas he flogged before continuing.

"Sir, why does he stop and rub the sub?"

"A couple of reasons: It keeps them connected; she feels his touch and hears his voice. It also helps the blood circulate."

"I've noticed the Dom moves spots, Sir."

"Right. You don't want to keep striking in the same place because it will cause bruises."

A shiver went through her body.

"I don't believe in bruising a sub. Some subs want it, and it takes a particular Dom to give that to them. I like knowing my sub has felt my flogger and doesn't need a visual reminder the next day, but she'll remember exactly where I caressed her skin."

Her toes curled as heat swept through her veins. How would it feel to know where he flogged her the next day? Her breath caught in her throat. She shifted in his lap.

"Someone is wiggly." His palms spread out over her abdomen.

"Sorry, Sir."

"Notice how the Dom is very careful where he flogs. He is only doing her shoulders, ass, and the back of her thighs."

"I did, Sir. Why?"

"To make sure he doesn't hurt her. He avoids the neck area, the kidneys, and lower back."

"Makes sense." Colby's hand moved, and Lara tensed.

"Easy, sweetheart." His voice was soft as he inched his hand under her top.

Lara could barely breathe as his fingers moved higher until they were right below her breasts, his nails teasing her sensitive skin.

"Sir?"

"Watch the scene."

Colby's voice had dropped a notch. He had to be

kidding. Lara bit her lip when his palm covered her left breast. He was touching her. Out in the open of the club. Why wasn't she telling him no? But this was no different from last Saturday, was it? Maybe because she wanted his touch more tonight.

When he switched to her other breast, her skin tingled with need. Her clit pulsed. She was getting turned on. That shouldn't have surprised her, but it did. Hell, her ex could barely get her wet and she loved him. Which proved the old saying that one shouldn't marry without sampling the treat. With Colby, all it took was his touch.

Cool air touched her skin, and she moved her head to look.

"No, sweetheart." Colby nipped her jaw. "Keep watching the scene."

"Yes, Sir." Lara swallowed, trying to control her breathing. What was Colby doing? One hand was on her breast, but where was the other one. The sub on the stage cried out, and the Dom stopped flogging her.

Lara kept her gaze on the Dom as he walked over to his sub and talked to her while rubbing her shoulders. The Dom smiled and set the flogger aside, and then began releasing the sub.

"I guess they're done," Colby said.

"Why did she cry out, Sir?" Lara was confused; she hadn't seen anything different in the way the Dom had flogged her to cause her to cry out.

"She climaxed."

"Oh." Lara ducked her head. It never occurred to her that someone could orgasm from a flogging.

"None of that." Colby tapped her chin.

"What, Sir?"

"Embarrassment. Nothing is taboo here."

"Not even ignorance, Sir?"

"You're not ignorant. You don't fully understand play yet, so none of that talk."

Lara wasn't so sure. The couple sharing the sofa with them stood, and Colby, instead of standing, maneuvered her and lifted her legs up so they were now resting on the sofa.

"Can you answer my questions truthfully?"

She stared at him. "I always do, Sir." Why was he questioning her?

"Did watching the scene arouse you?" Need coursed through her veins, and Colby chuckled. "Based on how pink your skin is, I'm going to take that as a yes. There is nothing wrong with that. How did you feel when I was playing with your breasts?"

"It was nice, Sir."

"Just nice? I guess I'll have to up my game."

Lara didn't like the wicked gleam in Colby's eyes, but she didn't know what to say. It was nice. "Your touch was soft and gentle, Sir."

A cry from across the room had her stiffening. Colby turned his head, and when he looked back at her, his lips were tilted up. "Just one of the subs on the spider web being spun around."

"Sounds dangerous, Sir." Spider web? Oh yeah, she remembered now, the big metal wheel that looked like a web.

"If it wasn't a Dom who'd practiced on it, yes. But Master Max is there watching and making sure nothing goes wrong. Now back to you."

Lara let out a sigh.

Colby held her gaze. "Sweetheart, if you don't want to play in the club, tell me."

"It's not that, Sir." She shifted on his lap. "I'm not sure

how to explain it, Sir."

"What is going through you mind?"

"I'm excited, but there is an underlying thread of unease."

"Do you know what is causing the unease?" His voice held concern.

"I..." Lara stiffened. "Damn," she whispered. *Appearances mean everything* flashed through her mind, again.

"Would you please share?"

She glanced around, there was no one near them. "Please understand, Sir, this might come out a little wrong. I trust you."

Colby lifted his hand and placed his palm on her cheek. Lara leaned into his touch. "I understand. And, for the moment, drop the Sir and talk to me."

"We've never really discussed how secure the club is." Would those who saw her here take it to the outside world? She knew the club had rules, but that didn't mean everyone followed them.

"Are you worried about your safety?"

"No. I said that wrong. I meant security wise. Remember what I said Tuesday."

His eyes narrowed. "There's the gate, and Ralph checks everyone in. Are you worried about someone getting into the club who doesn't belong?"

"There is that, but also outside the club." She let out a sigh. "After Keith told me they were watching me, I became worried about the club."

Colby froze. "Lara, you're safe here." His arms tightened around her. "As for outside the club, that's why we have the rules. You don't mention who you see in the club."

"I believe you. I've tried not to let his words get to me, but tonight...I'm sorry." She ducked her head. Why was she letting her family issues interfere with her relationship with Colby? Maybe because it was so ingrained in her to walk the straight and narrow?

"Sweetheart." His arm tightened around her shoulders. "There is nothing to be sorry for. I think we need to talk more about your family."

"Probably." He had a right to know what was going on. "My family would have rather I stayed married to my ex. They throw us together whenever they think they can, which is why I rarely visit my parents anymore."

Colby shook his head. "What is your brother's issue?"

"Keith thinks I need a keeper. He's a couple of years older and followed in our father's footsteps." She gave a bitter laugh. "Heck, so did Scott, my other brother. I'm the baby of the family."

"What about your mom? I can't imagine her putting up with all of this."

"Hazel Meyer never has a hair out of place, let alone shows any defiance toward her husband. The only reason I got to go to Berkeley was because I agreed to go to the business school. It backfired on my father, but he never realized it until I graduated."

"So they've always tried to stifle your nature?"

"A good way to put it." Lara stopped as Max walked up to them.

"Everything okay?" he asked.

"We're fine, but Master Max if you would pull up a chair for a moment and tell Lara about the security of the club and how only members can get in."

Max frowned, and he did something Lara didn't expect. He sat down on the floor next to the sofa. Max lifted his hand and waited. Colby nodded, then Max picked up her hand from where it rested on her leg.

"Lara, first off, everyone signs an NDA, and if anyone violated the NDA, they would be in a world of hurt. Trust me. Jordan, Damon, and I would never let that pass without serious consequences to the person. Second, no one gets in who doesn't belong. Not only is there a gate that is only opened with a code, but they have to check in with Ralph; if they're not on the list they're escorted off the property, not that anyone has ever gotten that far." Max chuckled. "Okay, one person, but that was Sierra, and she actually knocked."

Lara nodded, feeling a little better.

"If it helps to know, we're doing some upgrades that will include cameras not only at the gate but outside. The club's address is attached to my personal address, and unless you really know about the club, you won't find it. Plus, the computer system we use is air-gapped and encrypted."

"I see."

"The worry is still there." Max's gaze shifted from her to Colby. "What is going on?"

Colby glanced at her, and she let out another sigh. "My family." Damn, this wasn't how tonight was supposed to go.

"Her brother told her he was watching her," Colby clarified.

Max's gaze turned hard. "That is a good thing to know." Max squeezed her hand. "Lara, please don't be afraid to tell me if you're worried about someone who shouldn't be getting in. We're very diligent. But I appreciate the information."

"I've caused a problem, haven't I?" That was the last thing she wanted to do.

"No. You've made me aware there could be a problem." Max squeezed her hand. "I don't want you to worry about it. I'm very security conscious. Privacy isn't just the gate, but the NDA, the background check, and the classes."

"Thank you, Master Max." Her voice was soft.

Max squeezed her hand again before he rose to his feet. "Colby, demo on Saturday night?"

"Yes, I remember."

Max nodded and walked away.

"Demo?" Lara asked.

"I promised a month ago to do a flogging demo on Saturday."

"Do I get to watch?"

"If you want."

"I do. Are you good with a flogger?"

"The best." He leaned over. "If you were ready, I'd use you as my sub."

Lara squirmed. To feel the touch of Colby's flogger made her squirm in anticipation. "Maybe I am."

Colby grinned. "You need to walk before you can run."

Her lips turned up. "Then I guess you'll have to show me."

"It will be my pleasure." He dropped a kiss against her lips. "It's after ten, and I know you have to work tomorrow."

"Yes." She wished she didn't have to go to work tomorrow. That was a first for her.

"Come on. Let's get you home." He slid her off his lap, helped her to her feet, and guided her out of the club to the ladies' room. "Five minutes." Colby kissed her hand, then pushed her inside.

Lara was grinning when she opened her locker. She

grabbed her jacket, and that's when she looked down and gasped. Her top was totally open. How long had she been flashing everyone? Oh my God, she was exposed when Max talked to her. Her boobs right there in front of his face.

She laughed. Max never let on. Colby must have undone her blouse at some point, and she never noticed. Was that a bad thing? Nope, she decided. This was part of learning to walk. Lara slipped on her jacket and grabbed her purse.

Colby was waiting for her when she walked out. "When did you undo my blouse?" She needed to know.

"While you were watching the flogging scene. I kept you busy so you wouldn't notice."

"And I didn't."

"Does it bother you?"

"No." She grinned.

"Let's go." He held his hand out, and she put hers in it.

* * * *

Friday afternoon, Colby put the finishing touches on the flogger he wanted to use at the club tomorrow night. He laid it down and picked up his phone. While he'd seen Lara at the café this morning, he missed her. Plus, he wanted to take her out tonight.

Colby: *Dinner*

Lara: Sure. Where are we going?

Colby thought for a moment.

Colby: *Would you like to go out or stay in?*

Lara: *You choose.*

He let out a laugh. His independent woman was deferring to him more and more. He liked that.

Colby: *BBQ*

Lara: *Works for me*

Colby: *Pick you up at six*

Lara: *See you then*

Colby smiled when he saw all the emojis she put after her message. He made a reservation at the restaurant and began cleaning up his work area.

Chapter 9

Colby pulled up at Lara's home with a frown. There were two police cars there. He forced his panic into the pit of his stomach as he climbed off his motorcycle and raced up the steps. The door was partially open. He knocked. "Lara?"

"It's okay," she said softly to someone. "Come in, Colby."

He pushed the door open with his elbow. "What's going on?" Colby saw Logan standing near Lara. At least he knew Logan from the club. Lara was sitting on her sofa with her aunt.

Logan walked over to him. "Keep your cool, Colby," he said softly.

He frowned at Logan's words. "Are you hurt?" Colby asked, leaning around Logan to stare at Lara.

"I'm not hurt." She shook her head.

Colby looked at Logan. "Let's step outside," Logan said.

"Fine." Colby didn't like this, but he needed to know what was going on. He stepped out the door onto the stoop. "What the hell happened?"

"Lara isn't hurt. Shaken but not hurt," Logan said. "Someone broke into her home."

"I can see how that could be upsetting, but four officers? What aren't you saying?"

"That's not for me to say. We've gotten our report, so we'll leave."

Colby nodded, and they returned inside. The four officers left. "Lara?" Colby opened his arms.

In an instant, she was in his embrace. "I'm so glad you're here."

"So am I," Aunt Tammy said.

"Officer Wolfe said your house was broken into." Once Colby got more information from Lara, he'd talk with Logan again.

"Yes." A tremor shook her body. "This is crazy. The door was slightly open, but nothing was taken that I can see, and nothing is out of place, yet..."

"It's a violation." He glanced over his shoulder at the door. "How did they get in?"

"They had a key," Aunt Tammy said.

"What?" Colby stared at Aunt Tammy.

"Aunt Tammy, we don't know that."

"Pshaw. How else did they get in? The door lock is intact as well as the windows, and your alarm was off."

"I could have forgotten to activate it this morning," Lara said.

"Not likely," Aunt Tammy muttered.

"Are you okay, Aunt Tammy?" Colby asked, but he agreed with her. Lara was meticulous about her alarm.

"I'm fine. I was at my ladies group. They knew I wouldn't be home." She stood. "I'll head home now that you're here."

"Hold on," Colby said. He pushed Lara to arm's length. "Will you be okay while I check out your aunt's place?"

"Yes." Her voice was soft.

"No need," Aunt Tammy said.

"Every need," Colby said. He guided Lara over to the

sofa. "Sit down, and I'll be right back."

Anger simmered beneath Colby's skin as he escorted Tammy home and made sure no one had entered her home. It was clear.

"Take care of my girl, Colby," Aunt Tammy said.

"I intend to." Colby jogged down the steps and back up to Lara's place. She was sitting where he left her, gazing into space.

"I feel so violated," she said softly.

"Sweetheart." Colby closed the door and crossed over to her. He pulled her into his arms the second he sat down.

"Why would anyone break in and not take anything?"

Colby wondered about that too. "Are you sure nothing is missing?"

She nodded. "My TV is still here, my laptop is on the desk. Nothing looks out of place, yet I can't shake that something is off."

Colby didn't blame her. "Do you want me to check around?"

"I know the police did, but yes, please."

The tremor in her voice hit him hard in the gut. Colby let her go and stood. He checked her bedroom, bathroom, kitchen, and family room. Her place wasn't big. He frowned when he noticed the door in the kitchen to her garage was open. Her garage was on a lower level.

Quietly, he made his way over to her and leaned down. "Did you leave the kitchen door to your garage door open?" he whispered.

She shook her head. "I parked my car outside." Her eyes went wide.

"Go to your Aunt's," he ordered.

"Colby," she whispered.

"I can take care of myself, but not if you're here."

She shook her head. "There's no way out of the garage. We'd hear the door open, unless he comes up the stairs into here."

"What about the back yard?"

"There is that, but there's no way out. The fencing is too high."

"Go," he ordered as he heard a squeak.

Lara stood and went to the door. Colby turned and went into the kitchen, but he had a view of the garage door and waited.

He didn't have long; the door slowly pushed open and a person dressed in black and wearing a mask slipped out.

Two steps into the kitchen and Colby was on him, taking him to the floor. It wasn't much of a tussle. Colby had surprised the man.

"Here." Lara held out some rope.

"I told you to leave." He used the rope to tie the man up.

"I didn't listen." There was anger in her voice. "I also called the police."

"Which I thank you for." Colby looked up to see Logan and another officer. "Let him go. We'll take care of him."

Colby didn't like it, but he got up, and Logan reached down and hauled the man up to his feet.

Colby moved over to Lara and put his arm around her as Logan took the ski mask off the man.

"Lara, recognize him?" Logan asked.

"No." She glared at the man.

"Colby?"

"Never seen him before."

"Fine. We have you for breaking and entering. You have the right to..." The other officer started reciting as he led the man away.

"Any clue why he would be in your garage?" Colby asked Lara softly.

"Nothing there usually except for my car and some lawn equipment."

Logan started at them. "When you have a moment, go check and make sure nothing is missing. Charges will be filed for the breaking and entering, and I have your first report. We'll find out who he is and let you know."

"Thank you," Lara said quietly.

"I'll be in contact," Logan said and left, pulling the door closed behind him.

"Do you want to check the garage out?" Colby asked.

"Yes. I'll never be able to sleep if I don't." She shivered.

Colby led her to the garage door. Lara flipped the light switch. "Please stay up here until I call for you." He made his way down the stairs.

They weren't steep, which was good. At the bottom, he paused and looked around. Nothing seemed out of place to him, but he noted some hiding places. With caution, he stepped into the garage area and began checking it out.

Nothing. He breathed a sigh of relief. "You can come down."

Lara steps were soft as she made her way down the stairs. She paused and faced Colby. "Everything looks okay," she took the last step into the garage and began walking around. "Yep, nothing missing."

"Do you keep spare keys or anything like that hidden down here?"

She shook her head. "I think he must have been looking for a way out, and when there wasn't one, he waited until the police were done."

"Let's go back up." Putting his arm around her waist,

he guided her up the stairs. Once there, he shut and locked the door, with a mental note to buy and install a heavier lock.

"Not the way I planned for tonight to go," Lara said.

"Things happen." Which reminded him— He pulled out his phone and called the restaurant to cancel their reservation. "We can stay here and have pizza delivered, or we can go to my place and have pizza delivered."

Lara gave a laugh. "Pizza huh?"

"We have to eat."

"Graziano's is the best." Lara stood and went into the kitchen, returning with a menu in her hand. "What would you like?"

Colby looked over the menu. "Anything with meat on it, no olives or onions."

Lara called an order in and sat down next to Colby. He reached over and hauled her into his arms.

"I'm glad you're here," she said, resting her head against his shoulder.

"I am too." He dropped a kiss on top of her head and just held her in silence until the doorbell rang.

"Food," she said sitting up.

"I'll get it." Colby walked to the door and checked to see who it was. He opened the door.

"Hi," the deliveryman said. "Order for a large meat pizza, cheese bread, and for dessert, our special brownie delight." He held the food out.

"Thanks, Johnny," Lara said, smiling at the young man.

Colby handed the kid the money and took the food.

"Nice to see you, Miss Lara, enjoy." He turned and jogged down the steps.

"That smells delicious," Lara said. "Put it on the coffee table while I get plates and napkins."

Colby carried everything over to the table and set it down. Lara was right; this did smell delicious. She returned, and they ate.

"Well, since tonight is kind of messed up, what do you want to do?" she asked after they polished off dessert.

"It's fine." He helped her clean up and put the leftovers in the fridge. He'd noticed over dinner that Lara kept looking at the door as if she expected someone to be there. "Are you worried about another break-in?"

"Yes, no...Maybe." She let out a breath. "I'm glad you're here, but I don't get it. Why did he break in if he wasn't going to steal anything?"

"Maybe you got home before he could?"

Lara's nose scrunched up as she concentrated. "I was home a little bit earlier than normal, but still." She shivered.

"I'm sure it was just a random break-in and you surprised him." But he had to wonder. There were no broken windows or doors and there was the fact her alarm system had been turned off. "Why don't we find something on TV to watch?" He pulled her close once again.

"You pick." She handed him the remote. "I have several streaming services so I'm sure you can find something."

Colby scrolled through the channels and finally settled on an action/adventure movie. "Is this okay?" he asked as it started.

"It is. I love superhero movies." She settled against him.

Two hours later, Colby glanced down to see Lara was sound asleep. He wasn't surprised. The adrenaline spike was gone. He shifted on the sofa so she lay on top of him. He pulled the throw from the back and put over her. The next movie started as his eyes closed.

* * * *

Lara snuggled against something warm and somewhat hard. The heat is what kept her close. It might be late April, but they still had some cool nights. She curled her arm over... Hair tickled her skin. She froze and opened her eyes.

Twinkling green eyes were gazing down at her. "Good morning, sweetheart."

"Colby?" She was about to ask him what he was doing there when the events of last night came back to her. "You stayed?"

"You fell asleep on the sofa. I didn't feel right leaving you alone, so I carried you to bed."

Lara swallowed, glanced down, and blew out a breath. Okay, she was still wearing her panties. And Colby?

"Before you ask, yes, I undressed you, and I still have on my shorts. I didn't think you'd appreciate either of us being naked when you woke this morning." He tucked his chin down. "But I can remedy that if you want to play."

Want and need filled her veins until she remembered. "What time is it?" She twisted in his hold to look at the clock.

"About six," he said.

"I've got to get to the café." She'd rather spend the day in his arms, but she had a business to run. "I'm going to be late as it is."

"Then this will wait until later." He gave her a brief hard kiss and released her.

* * * *

Lara grinned as she pulled into the club parking lot. She'd seen Colby several times today, including a few hours ago when he loaded the hot boxes into her car. He'd spent last night with her. Her heart warmed. He'd held her all night, keeping her safe. Lara hated that she hadn't had time to spend with him this morning. Maybe tonight after they were done at the club. Actually, maybe she'd invite him back to her place tonight, and they could enjoy some sexy times in her bed.

She grinned at her thoughts. Colby was worried about how the burglar got into her place, so this morning, while she was at the café getting things ready for the club, he'd gone to the hardware store and picked up new locks. Not only for the front door, but the garage and Aunt Tammy's place as well.

Lara shook her head and told him he was overreacting, but she hadn't shut him down. While she was still processing what had happened yesterday, she had to agree that the door being unlocked bothered her as well.

As for the alarm, she'd called her alarm company asking them if there was a log of who used what code and what time. They were going to check for her and send her an email.

She grinned as she parked and saw Colby and Max come out the front door.

"Evening, Lara," Max said.

"Hi, Max," she replied. "Colby."

Colby's eyebrows rose, then he drew her into his arms and kissed her. Oh man, what a kiss. His tongue parted her lips and delved into her mouth. Her arms slid over his shoulders and around his neck. His palms cupped her ass, pulling her close, as the kiss went on.

A clearing of a throat had them pulling apart. Heat swept up her neck and face. "Sorry, Max," she said softly.

"Nothing I haven't seen before, but I figured you might want to get things set up before people start arriving."

"Yeah." She slid her hands from around Colby's neck, but her palms trailed over his collar bone and down his chest before she let her hands drop.

Within fifteen minutes, they had everything out of the car, and Lara was setting up while chatting with Sierra.

"I talked with Max. We're going to get you a store room where you can keep things you need here at the club so you don't have drag everything back and forth," Sierra said.

"Thank you. That would be nice." Lara thought about what she could keep here at the club.

"Are you excited about Colby's demo?" Sierra asked, picking up one of the mac and cheese bites and popping it into her mouth.

"I am. I saw some of his drawings of the floggers he makes." A tremor of excitement flowed through her veins.

"The demo is going to be first, isn't it, Max?" Sierra asked.

"Yes." He put his arms around Sierra's waist and pulled her against him. "Which reminds me. Colby, I gave you the night off since you're doing the demo."

"I didn't expect that," Colby said.

"I know, but there's enough of us here tonight to cover your shift."

"Thanks." Colby's gaze caught Lara's, and she ducked her head. The heat in his gaze burned her skin.

"You deserve it." Max guided Sierra away.

"Are you going to be okay with me doing this demo with Regina?"

"Yes." Lara smiled. He'd been worried, but she wasn't. Regina was nice and didn't have her sights set on Colby.

"I'm going to keep a spot open in the front just for you."

"You don't have to do that." A little thrill of passion flowed through her.

"I do." He cupped the back of her neck. "I want you close."

* * * *

Colby checked the scene one more time. His floggers were laid out on the small table, and he had lotion ready as well, along with a blanket. He'd talked with Regina about the scene. She was fine with his floggers and what he wanted to do.

The area was filling up, but Sierra made sure no one sat in the place he had reserved for Lara. Where was she? He looked over at the buffet, but he didn't see her. It was almost time. Regina climbed up on the stage.

"Do you want me nude, Sir?" she asked.

"If you want to be. I need access to your ass and shoulders." He could do that with a bra and thong on.

"I'm fine with it, Sir." She took off the short thin slip she wore and walked over to the St. Andrew's Cross and leaned against it so her back was to him.

Colby followed her. "Do you want me to restrain you?"

"Yes, Sir. It helps me get into the scene."

Colby fastened the restraints, making sure they weren't too tight. "Safe word?" While they'd already negotiated the demo scene, he always asked.

"Cotton."

His lips turned upward. "I'll start off slow."

"Yes, Sir."

"We're ready, Colby," Max said.

Colby turned to the gathered group. "Good evening." Colby spoke up so everyone could hear him. "Master Max asked me to do a flogging demo tonight. Regina graciously consented to be my sub." He pointed to her. "Flogging is something you need to practice before you try it on your sub or partner. You can practice on pillows, dummies, or

130

even the wall. I also suggest, as you get more proficient, you allow someone to flog you." A murmur went up from the crowd. "It's important you know how it feels so you know how your sub will feel. The power you put behind your strokes makes a difference."

He walked over to the table and picked up a small flogger. "This is a good one to start with." He flicked his wrist and snapped it against Regina's ass. She giggled. "This is a rabbit flogger. Very soft and low impact. Remember, if the flogger is new to you, try it out on yourself by hitting your upper arm or your thigh with it. If it hurts, think about how it will feel to your sub."

Movement caught his attention. Lara. She slipped onto the seat Sierra had saved for her. He froze for a second. She was wearing a pair of boy shorts and a gauzy looking shirt. Her nipples were hard against the fabric. His mouth went dry.

Colby set the rabbit flogger on the table and picked up the suede one. "Now this is a little heavier." He snapped it out and hit Regina's ass. She let out a sound, almost as if he surprised her. "This is good for a light to medium flogging. A lot depends on the power you put behind hit." He snapped it again, and Regina giggled. "That was a light strike." He did it again and she let out a moan. "That was harder."

"Excuse me, Sir?" a man in the audience said his hand in the air.

"Yes?"

"It didn't look like you changed anything."

Colby grinned. "It didn't look like it to you. Regina, can you explain to the Dom the difference in what you felt?"

"Yes, Sir. The first hit was more like a soft caress

against my skin; the second one was like a hand slap against my ass.”

“Thank you, Regina.” Colby ran his hand over her back. “While you didn’t see anything, every time you use a flogger, you have to remember the power you put behind it. For example.” Colby walked back to the table and picked up a bullhide flogger.

With care, he flicked it, and Regina yelped.

“This is bullhide; it is very heavy and thuddy, but a sharp thuddy.” Colby motioned the Dom forward. Colby handed him the suede flogger. “Use it against your arm.” The man did, then Colby handed him the bullhide one. The Dom tried it and winced.

“I see, Sir.” The Dom handed the flogger back and retook his seat.

“After the demo is over, please come up and try the floggers out. One thing I should mention: These floggers are all balanced for my hands, by that, I mean they’ve been made for me. The grip fits my hand, and the handle is balanced.”

Colby put the bullhide flogger down and picked up a leather one. He continued until he’d gone through all his floggers. He walked up to Regina. “Are you okay to do the Florentine?”

“Oh yes, Sir.”

The excitement in her voice made him smile. Colby glanced at Lara; she was leaning forward, watching.

“What I’m about to do is called a Florentine. I am able to do this only after years and years of practice, and it’s not for everyone.” Colby twirled the floggers, getting his mind into the game, and approached Regina.

The crowd let out an “ohh” as he flogged Regina, moving up and down her body. Shoulders, ass, and upper thighs. Colby didn't do it for long, just a few minutes, then he stopped.

There was silence for a few moments, then applause. Colby set his floggers down and grabbed the lotion. "I'm going to rub lotion into your skin, Regina."

"Yes, Sir." Her voice was soft, but she was still with him.

Colby rubbed the lotion in, his touch gentle, but impersonal. Once he was done, he grabbed the blanket and covered Regina and undid her restraints. She stepped back as he wrapped the fabric around her.

"Aftercare?" he asked, knowing she was one who didn't always want it.

"No need, Sir." Regina smiled at him. "I'm nice and tingly. I think I'll find a Dom to play with on the bondage system."

"Be careful, and thank you, Regina." He leaned over and brushed a kiss against her temple.

"It was fun to be your demo sub, Sir." Regina strode off the stage.

Colby chatted with the Doms, many with questions and others wondering about the floggers. Several wanted to understand more about the balance of the flogger he'd talked about, and Colby showed them. He also explained he'd made all the floggers he used tonight.

Several of the Doms smiled and said they would be contacting him. When the last Dom walked away, Colby put all his floggers back in his bag, and stored it in the cubbies by the bar before going to find Lara by the buffet. She was putting fresh trays on the table to replace the empty ones.

"How did you like the demo?"

Her eyes were bright. "It was very interesting."

"So is the outfit you're wearing." A blush warmed her cheeks.

"Do you like it?"

Colby drew her away from the table and pulled her into his arms. "I want to peel it off of you," he whispered.

Her smile lit up her entire face. "I really did enjoy your demo." She tilted her head. "I'd love it if you'd do it to me someday. It got me all hot and bothered."

If his cock wasn't already rock hard, it was now. His demo had lasted for over an hour, and Max had given him the night off. "What if I give you a personal demonstration? I can ask Max to reserve us one of the spanking benches."

Lara's eyes went wide. "Ummm…"

"I'm pushing." He ran his finger over her flushed cheek. While she didn't say it, the panic in her eyes said it all. It would take time for her to be comfortable playing in the club he reminded himself. "How soon can you leave?"

Desire flashed in her eyes. "Not for a little bit yet."

Colby bit back a groan.

Hannah approached them. "Sir, Ma'am."

Lara opened her mouth to correct her, but Colby shook his head. Lara frowned.

"Miss Lara, Sierra asked me to come over and ask if you would show me what needed to be done so you could leave with Sir Colby."

Colby glanced over his shoulder to see Sierra standing with Max, a wide grin on her face. They were setting them up, and he didn't mind.

"Oh, but—" Lara looked at him for help.

"Miss Sierra said she wanted to give you some time with Sir Colby and that I was to tell you the only right answer is yes."

Colby laughed, and Lara shook her head.

"Okay...Sorry, I don't know your name."

"Hannah, Miss Lara."

"First off, Hannah, it's Lara."

"I'll let you show Hannah what to do." Colby crossed the room to where Sierra and Max were standing next to the bar. "You two set this up."

"Guilty," Sierra said. "You two deserved some private time together."

"How do you know we're not getting it?" Colby asked.

"Logan told us about the break-in. He wanted everyone in the club to be on alert."

Colby frowned. "Have others from the club been targeted?" That would mean the break-in at Lara's wasn't random.

"No, but Logan isn't happy," Max said.

"Yeah." Colby had talked to him earlier in the day. "Apparently, the burglar had his lawyer waiting when they got to the station last night." Unwelcome news. "Maybe I should see if he has any new information." He turned.

Max's hand on his arm halted Colby. "Not tonight. Go spend some time with your lady tonight."

"Max is right, Colby. Lara was very into the flogging scene," Sierra said.

Colby let out a breath. "Quit playing matchmaker," he said softly to Sierra.

"Who me?" Sierra fluttered her eyes, and Colby laughed.

"Now you see why she always has me tied in knots," Max said.

"I do?" Sierra's voice held surprise.

Colby shook his head and walked back across the room to Lara and Hannah. They were chatting and laughing. "Ready?" Colby asked.

"I think so," Lara said.

"Please don't worry, Lara. I used to work at a restaurant; I know what to do," Hannah said.

Colby looped his arm around Lara's waist and led her away. If he didn't, she'd stand there another hour or more. Max and Sierra stood by the door with Colby's bag and Lara's purse and another bag.

"How did you get my things?" Lara's voice held surprise.

"Override for emergencies, like this one." Sierra grinned.

"Leave your bike in the lot. You can pick it up tomorrow or Monday, whenever you need it," Max told Colby.

"Thanks." Lara took her purse, and he took the bags and guided her out to her vehicle. "Will you allow me to drive?"

She stopped and looked at him. "Okay." She dropped the keys into his palm. Surprise jolted his body. "Thank you," he said. Colby blew out a breath as he opened the passenger door for her. He didn't want to argue, but he didn't want her driving. Once she was in, he dropped their bags in back before he got in.

He had to push the driver's seat back as far as it would go. Lara laughed.

"Hey, I'm a big guy."

She ran her hand over his arm. "Yes, you are." Her voice had dropped to a seductive level, and his cock pulsed.

Colby drove away from the club. "My place okay?" he asked.

"Yes. Hannah mentioned Logan was telling people about local break-ins and to be careful."

"Yeah, we're a community that protects our own."

Colby reached over and took her hand in his.

"So maybe it was just a random break-in," Lara remarked.

"Are you still worried?" She'd seemed fine this morning, but that didn't mean she wasn't concerned.

"A little bit. Today was bridge day at Aunt Tammy's house. They were still playing when I left, so that makes me feel better. Plus, the new locks. Thank you for that."

"Any idea why your alarm was off?" He still found that odd. He'd made sure it was set last night and again today when he left after installing the locks. Lara had given him a special code.

"I could have forgotten to set it."

"Not likely."

"I have to agree. I called the alarm company. They're going to send me a report on the codes used and when. Plus, I got the information on how to change my code."

"Good. What about the café?"

"Oh the café is fully alarmed as well."

"I'm glad you have a system at the café too." It bothered him that the man hadn't tried to take anything. Logan mentioned this morning the man had a long list of B&E's. But that was it. Interesting that he'd lawyered up so quickly.

Colby pulled up to his place. "Stay here," he said. Lara frowned at him, but she didn't move.

Chapter 10

Colby got out and jogged up the steps to his place. He automatically glanced at his mother's house. Security lights on, dark inside, and all looked well. After opening his apartment, he made sure everything was as it should be and no one else was in the apartment, then he went back down the steps to the car. He pulled their bags out of the car and escorted Lara upstairs.

"Are you always this protective?" she asked as he closed and locked the door.

"Yes. I won't risk you getting hurt." He ran his fingers over her cheek and saw her shiver.

"Colby," she started, then glanced at the floor. "I don't know what to say."

"You don't need to say anything." He led her into his bedroom and dropped their bags on the floor.

Lara took her jacket off and his mouth watered. "Damn, woman, you look good."

"Thank goodness for Sierra. She helped me pick it out.

"She did?"

Lara nodded. "I wanted to surprise you."

"That you did." He put his hands on her shoulders. "I want to peel the outfit off of you."

"Please." Her voice was soft, but passion flared in her eyes.

Colby undid the buttons on the blouse, sliding it off her

shoulders. Next came the boy shorts. He laid both on the chair and took in Lara from head to toe. She stood there in bikini briefs.

"I don't know how I made it out of the club without ravishing you."

Her skin flushed. "I want you to ravish me and more." Her voice was soft.

"Get on the bed while I gather a few things." He turned away, trying to keep his cock under control.

He opened his closet and looked at his toys there. He grabbed some items for them to use. When he turned back, Lara was lying on her side watching him.

"You are so damn beautiful." His dick pulsed with need and desire. He crossed to the bed and dropped the items on the side table. "Rabbit flogger, sensation mitt, and nipple clamps. Are you okay with all of it?"

She licked her lips. "Yes, Sir."

Colby removed his hoodie and removed the rest of his clothes. His cock was hard. "Keep that up and I'll have those lips wrapped around my dick."

"As if that would be a hardship, Sir."

Her words hit him like a rogue wave, almost sending him to his knees. Lara was so open and adventurous with him in private. "Not tonight." As much as he'd love to have her mouth on him, he wouldn't last more than a minute with her luscious lips wrapped around his cock.

Kneeling on the bed, he hooked his fingers under the fabric of the bikini briefs at her waist and peeled them off her. "Roll onto your stomach," he said as he grabbed the sensation mitt. Once Lara was on her stomach, he ran the mitt over her back.

"Ohhhh, that is nice, Sir."

"It's designed to awaken the nerves."

"It does that, Sir."

* * * *

Lara closed her eyes as Colby caressed her with the mitt. It was soft against her skin, almost like a caress. Slowly, the tension of the last few days dropped away. As he stroked her body, new sensations awakened.

Her pussy tightened when he caressed her ass. The flogging scene earlier this evening had gotten her hot and bothered. Heck, just putting on the leather outfit had awakened her libido.

She'd been worried about wearing the boy shorts and gauzy blouse, but Sierra convinced her it was the right look. Sierra had been right. The passion and fire in Colby's gaze when he saw her had made Lara grateful she'd been sitting down.

Her bones had turned to mush, and her brain had scrambled. At that moment, she'd wanted to be on that stage with Colby, feeling his flogger against her skin.

"Not falling asleep, are you?"

"No, Sir." She opened her eyes and found him staring at her with the rabbit flogger in his hand.

"Good. I'm going to swat your ass; tell me if it's too much."

"Yes, Sir."

Lara closed her eyes. The flogger hit her ass. Her body froze, and her eyes opened. "Oh my," she whispered. Colby swatted her five times before stopping and rubbing her butt with his palms.

"Talk to me. How did that feel?"

"I..." Lara tried to gather her thoughts. "I'm guessing thuddy would be right. It didn't sting. My butt feels hot, Sir."

Colby caressed her ass cheeks. "Yes, the flogging will

bring the blood to the area. Are you okay for more?"

"Please, Sir." She waited, then the flogger hit her upper thighs before moving back to her ass, then to her thighs again. Oh this was different. Her fingers curled into her palms, not in pain, but pleasure.

Her nerves tingled with each hit, and heat flowed through her veins like lightning. She let out a moan when Colby stopped.

"Sweetheart?" His hands massaged the areas he flogged.

"Don't stop, Sir."

His husky chuckle reached her ears. "I think that's enough for tonight."

"But." Lara let out a squeal when she was flipped onto her back. The intense look on Colby's face made her swallow her words.

"You have no idea of how sexy you are when my flogger warms your ass." He crawled up her body. "The soft cries you make, the way your skin flushes, and those cute little butt wiggles."

"Butt wiggles?"

"Yes." He brushed his lips over hers. "You wiggle your ass just a little after I hit it. Butt wiggles."

"Why did you stop?" She was curious. She'd been enjoying it, and apparently he had too.

"Because it's your first time being flogged, and I don't want to overload you." He sat up. Lara realized he was straddling her legs. "Besides, I want to play with these."

His palms covered her breasts and squeezed. "Oh yes," she whispered as he caressed her nipples. His skin against hers made her tingle in all the right places.

"Such pretty pink nipples." He pinched one.

Lara's back arched at the sharp pain and swift pleasure

that swept through her body.

"Shall we try these?" Colby reached over, holding a pair of nipple clamps. "These are beginner ones. I can tighten and loosen them very easily. What do you say?"

She squirmed beneath his body. His rigid cock pressed against her stomach. "Let's try, Sir."

He grinned and leaned down. His mouth covered her right nipple; he sucked and nipped. Heat swept from her breasts out through her body. Her clit pulsed with need.

"Please, Sir."

Colby lifted his head and put the first nipple clamp on. The clamp itself looked like a big tweezer. Once in position, he moved up a small metal disc.

"Ohhhh." The closer the disc got to the top, the more pressure the clamp put on her nipple.

"I think that's good. Let's do the other one." He repeated the process on her left nipple. By the time he was done, her breathing was choppy and fast. "I won't leave them on too long as you're not used to them."

He leaned down and brushed a kiss over her lips. "How do they feel?"

"Tight, Sir."

"Hummm." He shifted. "Maybe you need a little more stimulation." Colby slid his hand over her stomach to the top of her mound. His fingers parted her labia and found her clit.

"Damn." Her hips shifted up when he rubbed her clit.

"Now that got a reaction. I wonder how you would react if I clamped your clit?"

Her nipples throbbed as she shook her head. Clamp her clit? Oh no, that wouldn't feel good at all, yet she wondered how different it would be from her nipples. Her nipples didn't hurt; they pulsed with need.

"I see that thought makes you even more wet." He twirled his finger over her clit.

A tremor slid over Lara's skin. Her breath caught in her throat. How was this possible? She didn't have time to work it out as Colby took her clit between his thumb and forefinger and squeezed.

"Ahhhhh." She let out a cry as her toes curled, and her body shook. She was falling off a cliff into an abyss of pleasure.

"So beautiful." She barely heard Colby's voice with the roaring waves crashing in her ears. "Hold on, sweetheart."

Before she could process his words...he took the first nipple clamp off. Immense pleasure flowed followed by pain. A small cry left her lips. Her body continued to tremble. Lara tried to breathe through her mouth, but she couldn't catch her breath.

The sensations continued to flood her veins. Pleasure, some pain, and the immense feeling of flying free. When Colby released the second clamp, her body jerked against his.

"I've got you." Colby whispered as he pulled her into his arms, cradling her against his hot, hard body.

Lara laid against him, allowing herself to just feel. For the first time in her life, she felt free. Completely and totally free.

"Are you okay?" Colby asked sometime later.

"I'm in heaven." In a way it was true. Lara shifted, and her hand brushed up against his cock. Colby groaned. "I think I need to do something about this." Her fingers curled around his hard shaft.

Colby's fingers encircled her wrist. "You don't have to do anything."

She tilted her head and looked at him. There was

passion and need in his gaze. "But..."

His fingers covered her lips. "I'm fine, sweetheart."

She opened her mouth to argue, but the tightening of his lips told her not to. Lara wanted to give him the same satisfaction he'd given her, but for some reason, he wouldn't allow it. With care, she removed her hand from his cock. "Another time then."

"You can bet on it. I'm not done with you yet."

Lara grinned as he lowered his head and took her lips with his. Their tongues dueled as they tasted each other. Colby's hands weren't idle; they caressed the sides of her breasts.

"You taste like sin," he whispered against her lips.

"What does sin taste like?" She ran her palms over his back, enjoying the feel of his muscles playing under her skin.

"Like a sweet, decadent treat." His mouth nipped at her jaw.

"I think I like that." His fingers found her nipple, and she arched into his touch.

"I want to gobble you up." Colby shifted, and Lara parted her legs, cradling him between them. Her breath caught in her throat as his cock brushed against her pussy.

"I want that too."

His green eyes flared with desire. "Be careful what you wish for." Colby shifted his hips, and she let out a groan. "Condoms?"

"Drawer, but I'm on the pill, remember."

He grinned. "All my tests are negative. I showed you my medical report."

Lara giggle. "Romantic talk, Durham."

"Only the best." Colby rubbed his nose against hers. "Are you okay if I'm bareback?"

"Very much okay." She wiggled her hips.

"Vixen." His lips captured hers again as he shifted his lower body.

Lara breathed deeply through her nose as his cock penetrated her pussy.

Colby stilled and waited until her gaze met his. "How long has it been?"

"A while. I haven't dated much since my divorce. I was too busy running a business."

"I'll go slow."

"I don't want you to." Lara curved her legs around his ass. "I've waited long enough. I want you."

"Who has control in the bedroom?" His voice was husky with need, but his Dom tone was there too.

"I believe the sub has all the power, Sir."

He gave a rough chuckle. "Witch." Colby pushed into her.

Lara's mouth opened as her pussy stretched to accommodate him. Her legs tightened around him. "You feel so good." Her words were as choppy as her breathing.

"That's my line." Humor twinged his voice.

She could barely keep still as he thrust in and out of her. She dug her nails into his back as he took her. Her toes began to tingle. And before she realized what was happening, she climaxed.

"So beautiful." Colby's voice was soft as he nuzzled her neck before he stiffened and began pulsing inside her.

Lara's eyes drifted shut in bliss. This man was hers. At least for now. She'd think about forever later, because something inside her snapped into place in that moment. Colby shifted and flipped them so he was on his back.

"Rest now, sweetheart. Round two will be coming up soon."

Lara grinned and laid her head on his chest. What had she done to deserve a man like Colby in her life?

Chapter 11

"Now, what?" Lara muttered as she turned into her driveway. She'd driven Colby out to Wicked Sanctuary to get his bike, and he'd followed her back to her place.

Aunt Tammy was standing in her doorway, frantically waving. Lara parked in the driveway and climbed out of her car. She'd called her aunt this morning to let her know she'd be home in a bit.

Lara dashed up the steps with Colby right beside her. "Aunt Tammy, what's wrong? I told you to call me if you needed me," Lara said, speaking softly and touching her aunt's arm.

"I would have called, but I knew you were already on your way home. Your father and brother are inside." Aunt Tammy jerked her head toward the kitchen. "They won't leave." Her aunt's face was lined with worry, her voice full of tension.

Barging into her aunt's house as if they owned it and refusing to leave? Lara's blood pressure rose. She should just call the cops on them for trespassing and harassing an older person and a half-dozen other crimes. But she took a deep breath instead. This was family. She would deal with it privately. "It's okay. I'll take care of this." She guided her aunt inside and had her sit down on the sofa. She glanced at Colby. "My fight," she whispered.

He gave her a sharp nod and a look that said he had her

back no matter what. "I'll stay with her."

"Thank you." He understood. Lara straightened her shoulders and marched into the kitchen. Her brother and father sat at the table. Interesting that her other brother wasn't involved in this, at least not yet.

"It's about time," Keith said.

"Where were you last night?" her father, Lawrence, demanded.

"None of your business." Lara put her hands on her hips. "Why are you bothering Aunt Tammy?"

"We're not. We wanted to talk to you," her father said. "But you weren't home."

She planted her feet and crossed her arms. "We've got nothing to talk about. Now get out. You will not barge into Aunt Tammy's home ever again."

"Actually, we do have something to talk about." Her father stood up. Not a strand of gray hair out of place.

"I doubt it, but in any case, we will do so outside. I won't tolerate this invasion of Aunt Tammy's privacy."

"Oh, I don't think this is something you want your neighbors hearing."

"You mean *you* don't want them hearing. What is it? Spill it, then get out."

"Keith and Walter tell me they tried to help you rid yourself of the bikers that frequent your café."

"They gave some of my customers a hard time, and I had them removed." Lara put her hands on her hips.

"That doesn't say much for your business if you have allowed riff-raff in."

"That *riff-raff*, as you call them, are kind, friendly, paying customers. I won't have them ridiculed in my shop."

"It doesn't look good to have those kind of people hanging around your café. It's a blemish on our family name and is bad for appearances."

"I don't care one whit about our family name or appearances. I care about my customers."

Her father huffed. "If you won't follow even a modicum of sensibility, I'll have to make you. So here's the deal. My bank holds the loan for your café. If you don't stop allowing those horrible bikers in, I'll call in your loan."

Lara's jaw dropped. She closed her eyes and took a deep breath. *Don't let emotions get in the way. They'll use it against you.* "You can't do that. It's written into the loan contract." Thank goodness she'd had the foresight to have that added.

"You need to get rid of the bikers, Lara," her brother said. "They're hurting the family."

"Oh really?" She glared at her brother. "The only one hurting the family name is you and your prejudice. The bikers are fine. And I'm not about to ask them to stop coming into the café."

"Then I'll sell the loan to another bank," her father said.

Lara shook her head. "You can try, but it's also in my contract that you cannot sell the loan without giving me ninety days written notice and a chance to pay it off before it is sold." She was tired of this crap.

She never should have used her father's bank to finance the café, but at the time, it was her best option. Now, the business had established an excellent credit history and profit margins, so she could easily find another bank to carry the loan, maybe not with as favorable terms, but the café was doing well financially, so if she had to pay more on a mortgage, she would.

"There are ways around the contract," her father said.

"Do you really want this to become a court case with

all the publicity that will go with it?" She wasn't bluffing. Even if it meant taking out a second mortgage on the café, she wouldn't let her father control her business. Enough was enough.

"Get rid of the bikers, Lara, or face financial ruin." Her father stormed out of the kitchen.

"Dad's not kidding," her brother said, following their dad.

"I don't care. When will you and Dad learn that it's my café? And what the hell is all this bullshit about family name and crap. What do you two have against the bikers?" She couldn't figure that out. She'd never seen the bikers bother anyone, never heard anyone talk against them.

"It's none of your business. Just get rid of them." Keith stormed out.

Lara left the kitchen to find her aunt crying on the sofa. "Aunt Tammy." Lara sat down next to her. "Don't let them upset you."

"But everything you've worked for."

"They can't touch it." Financially, they couldn't, but in other ways, maybe they could. Would her father want that much publicity? Negative publicity, because that's what it would be. He was so worried about the family name.

Her aunt kept crying.

"Honestly, they can't touch me. They can make things difficult, but I can survive them."

"Really?" Her aunt looked at her with a tear stained face.

"Yes." Lara grabbed some tissues and handed them to her aunt. "Where is Colby?" she asked.

"He stepped outside."

Crap. Lara stood and crossed to the door. Thankfully, her father and brother were gone; Colby was just outside her front door talking on the phone. He waved at her, indicating he'd be right there. She nodded and stepped back inside.

"How about some tea?" Lara really wanted something stronger.

"That sounds lovely," Aunt Tammy said, smiling.

Putting her arm around her aunt's shoulders, Lara guided her into the kitchen and had her sit at the table while she put on water for tea. Colby walked into the kitchen just as she poured her aunt a cup.

"Tea?" she asked holding up the kettle.

"No, thanks, sweetheart." Colby took a seat at the table. "Tammy, I don't want you to worry." Colby patted the back of her hand.

Aunt Tammy gazed up at Colby, her smile spreading across her face. "You'll take care of my Lara, won't you?"

Lara wanted to tell her aunt she didn't need to be taken care of but left it alone. Her aunt was worried enough.

"I will always take care of Lara."

After tea and an attempt at lighter conversation, Lara and Colby walked into her home. "I'm so angry," Lara said, tossing her bag from last night into her bedroom.

"I don't blame you." He stared at him. "I might have overstepped, but I heard what your father was saying. I called Jordan since he's a lawyer."

Lara froze. "You shouldn't have done that without taking to me first."

Colby looked surprised, and Lara didn't blame him. She didn't generally question his actions.

"You're not angry?"

"I am. You did overstep, but in this case, it was warranted. What did Jordan say?"

"He said if your father does anything, bring the

contract and any correspondence to him, and he'll look into it."

"I don't think my father is that stupid. It would sully the family name." She grimaced. "But anything is possible. I have no idea why my family dislikes the bikers."

"Because they're attached to me?"

"What?" Lara stared at him.

"I own the leather shop. The guys are in there all the time, and they come to your café. If it wasn't for my shop, the bikers wouldn't be there. What is there for them on this side of town? Not much."

"Is there something you're not telling me?" There had to be more than that. Why would her family want him gone?

He shook his head, but she had a feeling he was holding something back. "If they get rid of the bikers, in a sense, they could get rid of me."

"I'm not allowing you to go anywhere." Lara put her arms around his neck.

"Well, that's good to know." He pulled her close to him. "What are you going to do?"

"See if my father follows up on his threat, though I doubt he will." She let out a yawn.

"Sleepy?"

"Someone kept me up late last night and woke me early this morning."

"That I did."

Lara laughed. "It was a delightful way to wake up."

"I'll have to do it again."

"How about right now?" She took his hand and drew him to her bedroom with his husky laughter filling the air.

* * * *

Monday morning, Lara arrived at work on pins and

needles, but the day proved to be a normal day, as did the rest of the week. Nothing from her father or brother, but she wasn't quite ready to decide she was out of the woods yet.

She'd gotten the report from the alarm company Friday morning and found someone *had* used her code. Lara had already changed it, but she let Officer Wolfe know what the alarm company had said and who knew the code.

The officer had also given her an update on her case. The perpetrator had posted bail, with a hearing in several months. But since nothing was taken, he doubted much would happen with the district attorney. Lara thanked him and let the matter drop. It wasn't worth pursuing. Colby might not agree with her, but Lara had a feeling it was a dead end. Now that she had new locks and alarm codes.

Colby had also been worried that, maybe instead of taking anything, the robbery was a cover for placing something inside her apartment. Logan had given him the name of a security company who came over and swept her duplex. No bugs and no cameras, so the break in was still a mystery.

Colby stopped by every day that week, actually more than once a day. He'd come in the mornings, then stop by in the afternoons. Lara grinned. Everyone was getting used to him walking in and giving her a kiss. She grinned as she cleaned up.

"I'd grin too if I had that sexy man in my life," Eve, her employee, said.

"Thanks." Lara couldn't believe how lucky she was to have Colby in her life. They'd played last weekend at his place, and this week at hers. It was fun and exciting and darn right sexy.

The café door opened, and Sierra and Crystal walked in.

"Hey, ladies," Lara called out.

"Hey." They both smiled.

"Please tell me you have a piece of German chocolate cake left for me?" Crystal asked.

"Of course. Sierra?"

"Boston cream if you have any."

"I do." There was one in the fridge. "Go sit down, and I'll get it for you." Lara went into the kitchen and plated the desserts before taking them out to the women.

"You are a life saver," Crystal said, digging into her cake.

"Do you want coffee or anything?" she asked as Eve bustled up with two glasses filled with water. "Thanks, Eve."

"Water is perfect," Sierra said. "Lara, will you sit down for a minute?"

Since it was close to closing time, there wasn't much to do. "Sure." She sat. "What do you need?"

"Last Saturday worked out perfectly, and Max and I were wondering if you could do it every Saturday night."

Lara was taken back. "Every Saturday." It would be work.

"Yes. The club members are enjoying the perk and so are we."

"I'd have to work out new costs since we only talked about doing it once a month. Every week can be done, but I'll need to hire more help."

"Understood. Work out the costs and we can talk? Are you coming to the club with Colby tomorrow night?"

"I'm not sure." They hadn't talked about it. "I know he's working tonight."

"Yeah and tomorrow. I can't believe how busy the club has gotten."

"I think Lara's food has something to do with it," Crystal said.

"My food?" Lara stared at her. "It's nothing special."

"That's where you're wrong," Sierra said.

"I have to agree," Crystal commented.

Lara sat back in her chair. She served basic food, nothing fancy.

"Forgive me for overhearing," Eve said. "But they're right. Haven't you noticed how busy we're getting?"

"Until I get a new person onboard and trained, I have increased yours and Megan's hours. So yes, I've noticed, but..." Her voice trailed off. "I see what you mean."

"I've mopped up and everything, and I'm going to leave. I'll lock the door behind me so you ladies can talk," Eve said.

"I didn't realize people from the club were coming in here," Lara said.

"Not only them, but people they work with and other friends," Sierra said.

Lara hadn't really looked at the tallies this week. She put the money in the bank, scanned the receipts, and sent it over to her accountant. Accounting was not her strong suit. She much preferred her history and culinary classes.

"Word of mouth is a great thing," Crystal said.

"I guess it is." She was stunned at the turn of events. "I can work out some numbers and set up a time to talk with you and Max." She rubbed her finger over her cheek. "Also, I'll need help; I can't see Max allowing one of my employees access to the club."

"Yeah, we'll need to discuss that."

Crystal's phone beeped, and she let out a groan. "The lord and master calls."

"I'm going to tell Jordan you said that," Sierra laughed.

"You do, and I'll tell Max about your secret DVD stash."

"Bitch."

Lara loved the friendship between the women. Which reminded her. "I haven't seen Tessa lately."

"Yeah, her mom is visiting, and Tessa wanted to keep a low profile right now. Not that her mom isn't aware of what went on after all the crap with her father..." Sierra waved her hand in the air.

What was it about fathers and brothers? Lara didn't understand.

"I better go." Crystal stood and looked down at her empty plate.

"Go, I can take care of it." Lara stood. "You too, Sierra."

"You're a doll." Sierra dropped a twenty on the table.

"Sierra, that's way too much," Lara said.

"It's perfect."

Lara unlocked the door, and the women walked out. After relocking the door, Lara picked up the money, the empty plates, and glasses. It only took her a few minutes to clean everything up and get today's money in the bag for the bank.

Lowering the metal gates around the doors and windows, Lara set the alarm and went out the back door. She drove to the bank and deposited the money. Once at home, she scanned the receipt and looked at the totals for this week.

Oh my, she was making almost double the amount she made three months ago. That was amazing. Tomorrow was inventory day, but she had noticed today they were getting low on items that usually lasted longer.

She made a note on her calendar to call her accountant

next week and discuss everything. Next, she went through her spreadsheet on the food and supplies she'd been using at the club.

It wasn't super expensive, but she could see that doing it each week would mean making sure Megan and Eve both worked on Saturdays, and she'd recently hired a person who'd asked for time to finish up with their other job. She was in communication with him and setting up a training time. She wrote down several figures.

It wasn't that she was a bad business person; she wasn't. She just sometimes didn't know how to value things like her time. Colby would know. She picked up the phone and called his shop.

"Durham's Leather Shop, this is Colby, how may I help you?"

"Hey, sweet guy, how about dinner before you have to go to the club tomorrow night?" She kept her voice light and flirty.

"Well, sweet cheeks, that sounds grand. Will you come to the club with me after?"

"Aren't you working?"

"I am, but having you there makes for a better night."

Lara shifted in her seat. "I wish you could come over tonight."

"I can be there after my shift."

"What time do you get off?"

"Midnight."

"I'll be waiting."

* * * *

"You said you wanted my advice on something," Colby asked over dinner Saturday night. They really hadn't had a chance to talk much on Friday, but she mentioned needing his advice.

157

"Yes." While they'd spent Friday night together, Colby had rushed off to his shop and her to her café this morning. "Max and Sierra have asked me to cater every week at the club."

He frowned. "That's a lot of work."

"A bit. I've hired another person at least part-time to help at the café."

"What about at the club?"

"The night of your demo showed me I don't have to man the table all night, but I would prefer to have someone there. Sierra had Hannah restock food after we left, and it all worked out well. But I will discuss using Hannah with Max and Sierra."

"So why are you hesitating?"

"There's a reason I have an accountant, and I've made an appointment to see her next week. But I wanted to give Max and Sierra an answer, and I'd like a second set of eyes on my cost estimates."

"I thought you went to business school."

"I did, but honestly, now I have to value my time along with everything else. That's the part I have the hardest time with."

"Good thing you have me around." He flexed his fingers. "This isn't something we can do over dinner. How about I come by tomorrow afternoon and we go over everything, and I'll cook you dinner?"

"I'd love that."

"Good. Now finish eating."

* * * *

Colby walked around the club. He had the late shift tonight. Midnight to four am. He'd sat with Lara, and they'd watched some scenes together. Tonight, she'd been dressed in a black sports bra and boy shorts.

158

While she was getting comfortable showing more of her body, she wasn't comfortable playing in the club yet, and he wouldn't pressure her. It didn't stop him from touching her. They'd come in separate vehicles, and he saw her off at eleven, then waited until she texted him she was home before he went back into the club.

Now, it was three. Almost time to close up. There were only a handful of people left, including Damon and Tessa.

"Not a bad night," Damon said, walking up to him.

"No."

"I'm going to close down early. This will give us time to make sure everything is cleaned up and get home before sunrise."

Colby laughed. Since it was spring, the sun was coming up earlier and earlier. "Sounds good to me. Where's Tessa?"

Damon pointed to one of the sofas where Tessa was curled up with a blanket over her. "She worked today but wouldn't stay home. She crashed about an hour ago." Damon walked away and started telling those left they were closing down.

While he did that, Colby took the cleaning wipes and began wiping down the equipment. When Damon returned, there were only two stations left to do.

"You're quick," Damon said.

"Most were already cleaned. The club members are very good about cleaning up after themselves."

"They are. If you don't mind my asking, how is training with Lara going?"

"Good." Colby eyed Damon. "Has she said something?"

Damon shook his head. "We've got a new batch of members coming in next month for classes, and we need to figure out who is available for training."

"I'd rather not train anyone."

"Kind of figured that. Since we usually use DMs for training, something has to change."

"What about using some of the unattached Doms?"

Damon looked at him. "I know Noah and Oliver have been members for years, and they play with the club subs. They never bring anyone. I don't believe either is married."

"They're not." Damon rubbed his chin. "I'll talk with Max and Jordan; that might be a solution. Thanks."

"Anytime."

They finished up, and Colby changed clothes and went back and waited while Damon did the same and picked up Tessa. Colby held the door and made sure it was locked as they walked out. He also opened the door so Damon could put Tessa in the car.

"Night, Colby," Tessa said softly, looking over Damon's shoulder as he placed her in the vehicle.

"Night, Tessa." He waited until Damon closed the door. "Have a good evening, Damon."

"What's left of it."

Colby climbed on his motorcycle and rode away. On the ride home, he thought about what he'd said to Damon about training. He didn't want to train anyone else, but what if Lara could never play in the club?

His gut tightened. How important was playing in the club to him? Before he met Lara, he would have said very important, but now? He wanted her to be comfortable, and if that meant she couldn't play in the club, so be it. She didn't seem to mind coming to the club and waiting and watching as he worked. He could play in the privacy of their home.

Their home? Yes, he was thinking about a permanent

relationship with Lara. He'd never enjoyed being with a woman as he did with her.

When Colby parked his bike, a shadow caught his eye. Without thinking, he swung his helmet. He caught the person unaware. The helmet crashed into the person's face.

"Fuck."

The voice was male. Colby went into a fighting stance, but he didn't have to worry. The guy was already running away. He ran to a car idling a few houses down, jumped in, and they took off.

It was too dark to see the make of the car, let alone get the license plate number. With a sigh, Colby climbed the stairs to his apartment. Burglar or something else? Once inside, he checked his apartment. Nothing had been disturbed or was missing. He called the police to report what had happened.

They took a report over the phone since no one was hurt. Well, he wasn't, but he was pretty sure he heard bones crunch when he hit the other guy. Colby also texted Logan to let him know he'd filed a report.

But Colby couldn't get it out of his mind that this wasn't random. It felt like the man had been waiting for him, especially at this time of the morning. Admittedly, his neighborhood wasn't the safest, but still. No one ever bothered him or his mother.

Mom? Colby sprinted out of his apartment to her house. It was locked up tight and nothing looked disturbed. Using his key, Colby let himself in. He tiptoed to his mother's room to find she was sound asleep.

He took a breath in relief and left as quietly as he came in. Back in his apartment, he yawned as he walked into the bathroom and stripped. After a shower and drying off, he fell into bed. It had been a busy day. He'd puzzle out his mystery attacker later.

* * * *

Lara made some iced tea for herself and Colby, and she had some cookies. She'd run to the grocery store Sunday morning. Colby said he would cook for her, but he was helping her out. So, she'd picked up everything to make spaghetti with meat sauce and garlic bread. Since the café was closed, she grabbed a couple pieces of cheesecake for dessert from the store.

The doorbell rang, and she checked to make sure it was Colby before she opened the door.

"Hi," she said as her pulse kicked up at the sight of him.

Colby pulled her into his arms, and his lips captured hers. Heat flowed through her veins. Lara wrapped her arms around his neck, holding him close.

"Wow," she said when he lifted his head.

"Sorry. I couldn't wait to taste you." He kept his hands on her waist as he walked her backward, pushing her front door closed behind them.

"Nothing to apologize for." She loved his passion. There was so much to love about Colby. Her thoughts froze. Love? Was she in love with Colby? The truth smacked her upside her head. While she'd thought she'd loved Walter when she married him, it was nothing like what she felt for Colby.

How would he feel if she couldn't play in the club? Lara's gut churned. She still didn't fully understand why she didn't want to play in the club. She needed to talk with someone about that. Maybe Sierra or Crystal or even Tessa. The club was important to Colby, so if there was any chance for them as a couple, she'd need to find a way to make it work.

162

"I've got some iced tea and cookies in the kitchen so we can talk."

"All right." He slowly let her go. "But after our talk, you're all mine."

Excitement shot up her spine. "Of course. Plus, I have stuff to fix us a quick meal later."

"All right," Colby said after she sat down. "Tell me how much it cost you to cater to the club?"

"I'm embarrassed to say I never really figured it out, since I had everything Max wanted." She ducked her head. "I guessed at what to charge Max."

Colby stared at her. "All right. Let's break this down. How much food do you bring to the club?"

"I've been bringing enough appetizers and desserts for people to have two each, the cookies, enough for three per person."

He scribbled on the paper she'd give him. "How much does each item cost you?"

"Depends, the appetizers about a hundred for a box of two hundred, the desserts run from a dollar per piece to two dollars."

"What have you been charging Max?"

"Three hundred."

Colby's pen flew over the page. "Sweetheart, you're barely breaking even."

"I never really noticed. Because I order what I use in the café, I wasn't paying that close of attention. My accountant pays all the bills."

"You said you had an appointment with your accountant; would you mind if I went with you?"

Lara sat back in her chair. Her first reaction was a big fat *no*. That was a gut reaction because of her family always wanting to step into her business. But this was Colby. She trusted him in more ways than one, and he ran his own successful business.

"I'm overstepping, forget it."

"No." Lara put her hand out to him.

"I don't want you feeling uncomfortable."

"I'll admit it took me a minute, and my gut reaction was to say no." She squeezed his fingers when he put them in hers. "Not because we have a relationship or anything like that, but because my family has tried to interfere with my business and tried to take things over more than once."

"I want to help you; I also want to make sure you're making money from catering to the club. Right now, I can tell that you need to raise your price." He paused. "I'll talk to Max."

"No, thank you. I appreciate your help, but this is my business. I'll talk to Max."

"All right." Colby grinned. "Now that you've decided to let your accountant weigh in, I think we're done." Colby pushed the paper and pen away, then drew her out of her chair. "We play."

Chapter 12

"You look like you're in shock," Colby said as they left her accountant's office Wednesday afternoon.

"I am." The amounts her accountant threw out at them still bounced around in her head.

"I would think you'd be happy you're doing so well." Colby helped her into her car, then climbed behind the wheel.

"I am. I just didn't expect..." She shook her head. "I knew the café was doing well, but not *that* well."

"Your accountant agrees with me about what to charge the club."

"Yes, but it seems like a lot. I'm mean I'm raising the price by forty percent."

"I bet Max doesn't even blink an eye at it." Colby pulled up in front of her duplex.

"I hope you're right." She climbed out of her car and looked at him. "Are you coming in?"

"If you want me to."

"Yes, I need to talk this out with someone."

He guided her inside, and Lara poured them both something to drink and put some cookies on a plate.

"I never thought to ask, do you need to get back to your shop?" she asked.

"No. Kase and Issac can take care of the store for the rest of the day."

"All right." She put the file of papers from her accountant in front of her and opened it.

"My accountant suggested expanding, but I'm not sure how to do that without moving, and that would be a hassle."

"I noticed the ice cream shop next to you is closing," he said.

"Yes. The owner is up there in age. Mr. Torrino said his kids aren't interested, and he wants to retire."

"Does Mr. Torrino own the building?"

"I believe so."

"Maybe check with him and see if he'll sell to you." Lara tilted her head. "I can talk with Zeke since he's in construction, but he could probably remove the wall between your café and the ice cream shop to open the space up. You could expand your freezer space and your counter and just about double your seating area."

Lara rubbed her forehead. "That's a lot."

Colby smiled. "It is, but think about it. Look how popular you are. The only time there's an empty table at the café is late in the afternoon when you're getting ready to close."

"True." Lara couldn't believe how busy she'd gotten, and based on the information her accountant had given her, she needed to do something with the money. And the best thing to do with profit was to plow it back into the business. "Thank you for coming with me and helping me understand all this."

"If it doesn't upset you, I agree with your accountant that you need an onsite bookkeeper."

"She's right. I don't know why I didn't think about that sooner."

"By expanding, you can create a small office for them to work in with a computer and everything they need."

"It's all so much." Lara shook her head.

"One step at a time." Colby squeezed her hand. "First step, check on the sale of the ice cream shop and go from there."

"Right." Lara took her pen and began making a list. This was her go-to for figuring out what needed to be done when.

* * * *

Lara walked around the club on Saturday. She'd talked with Max on Thursday about the cost of catering, and he agreed without blinking an eye, just as Colby had said. Max agreed that having one of Lara's employees come to the club wasn't viable, but someone from the club could help her.

On Friday, she and Max talked with Hannah since she'd helped before. Hannah was only too happy to pitch in. When Lara offered to pay her, Hannah told her no; it was fun to do the food, and she didn't want to be paid. Lara wasn't sure how she felt about that, but she'd figure something out. Max told her he'd make some sort of arrangement with Hannah in lieu of pay, which made Lara feel better.

"Hello, my beautiful lady." Arms slid around her waist from behind, and she was pulled against a warm chest. The scent of leather and oil told her it was Colby.

"Done for tonight, Sir?"

"Yes." He nuzzled her neck. "You still want me to flog you here in the club tonight?"

Lara swallowed as her gut clenched. "Yes, let's do it, Sir." This was important to Colby. While she still hadn't figured out why having him flog her in the club bothered her, she wanted to try.

His arms tightened around her waist. "Station four is

open; why don't you go over there while I get my bag?"

"Yes, Sir." Lara made her way over to station four. Spanking bench. That shouldn't be too bad. Colby arrived and set his bag on the floor.

"I'll get things set up." He dropped a kiss on her lips before he mounted the stage. Lara watched him move the spanking bench, open his bag, and take out the rabbit flogger and the suede flogger, lotion, and he'd grabbed a blanket.

He turned to her and held out his hand. Lara took a deep breath and placed her hand in his. Once in the scene area with him, her heart sped up. There was something to be said about getting into the right head space.

"We haven't used a spanking bench before." He guided her over to it. The wooden contraption made her think of something out of the 1800s they used to punish people on. "Basically, you kneel here." He patted the low padded bench. "Then lean over. This will support your upper body. There is a place for you to rest your arms and head."

"I see, Sir." She did. A tremor of unease slid up her spine.

"Since this is your first time, I won't restrain you."

"Thank you, Sir." They'd played at his place with restraints while he flogged her ass. But here in the club... Another shiver went over her skin. *Appearances.* The word slipped into her mind, and she tried to push it away.

"Ready?"

Lara hesitated, and Colby's eyes narrowed. "Yes, Sir."

His forehead creased with a frown. "Lara, if this isn't what you want, we don't do it."

She opened her mouth and closed it. "I'm fine, Sir."

"Safe word?"

"Cookies." It was something she wasn't liable to

scream out during sex, and she could remember it. Lara stepped up to the bench and knelt down.

The padding cradled her knees. Nice. Colby helped her lay down. The spanking bench was set at the perfect height for her to bend at the waist without putting pressure on her stomach.

She laid her arms alongside her body on the shelves, as she thought of them, and laid her head on the small pillow.

"Breathe, sweetheart." Colby rubbed her back even though she still had a sports bra on.

Lara took a shaky breath as she watched Colby walk over to the table where he'd set up his floggers and pick up the rabbit flogger.

His fingers caressed her upper thighs and played with the elastic waist band on her boy shorts. "I'm going to pull these down around your knees."

"Yes, Sir." Her voice came out soft and shaky.

The cool air caressed her ass as he pulled her shorts down. Every muscle in her body tensed up. *Breathe, relax,* she told herself. *Pretend we're at home, and you're bent over the sofa arm.*

Colby trailed the tails of the flogger over her ass, up and down her ass crack, making her shiver at the sensation. So soft and sensual. Her limbs relaxed.

She tensed with the first swat and blinked at the pain. Not that there hadn't been pain in the past when he flogged her, but he was using the rabbit flogger. That shouldn't hurt. *Relax.* Easier said than done. She couldn't get out of her own head and enjoy what Colby was doing to her.

After the fifth swat, Colby stopped and rubbed her ass. "Sweetheart, you're way too tense." He continued to massage her ass.

"Sorry, Sir." She didn't know what else to say.

Colby's concerned face came into her line of vision. "Nothing to be sorry about. You're not enjoying this, are you?"

"I..." Tears of frustration filled her eyes. Why couldn't she do this? She was failing. She hated failing at anything, but she was also disappointing Colby. The pain in her chest felt like a dagger through her heart.

"Sweetheart." Colby motioned to someone who took the flogger from him and handed him a blanket. He stood and the blanket covered her backside. "Can you rise up on your knees?"

"Yes, Sir." She hated that tremor in her voice. Using her arm, she pushed up and got to her knees. Colby was right there, gathering the blanket around her before he lifted her into his arms.

He carried her off the stage and into the aftercare area. "I'm going to set you on the sofa, clean up our scene, and I'll be back. Don't move."

She nodded and watched him walk away through her tears. She ruined this for him. She was a failure. Big time.

* * * *

"I'm sorry," Lara said, blinking back her tears. Why couldn't she stop the waterworks? This was so unlike her.

"Sweetheart." Colby put his arm around her shoulders as he walked her into her duplex.

"I'm letting you down." She hung her purse on the coat tree. "Don't say I'm not. I saw the disappointment in your eyes." Why couldn't she drop her inhibitions in the club? It wasn't like anyone cared. Heck, only her ass had been bare.

"You could never disappoint me, sweetheart. We're still trying to figure us out. Whether or not you are comfortable playing in the club is secondary."

"It doesn't feel right to make you wait."

Colby cupped her cheek. "I'll wait however long you need."

"I don't deserve you." Lara couldn't believe how giving Colby was.

"I think you mean I don't deserve you." His lips turned up. "Now, let's go to bed." Colby guided her into her bedroom.

An hour later, Lara was still awake. She'd let Colby down tonight. Monday, she'd call Sierra and see if they could plan some time to talk privately. After the café closed. Lara needed to figure out why playing at the club was such a hard sell for her.

* * * *

A little over a week had passed since the night they played. Lara and Sierra had talked and talked. Sierra's experiences in the club, good and bad, helped Lara understand more. Lara was also beginning to wonder if there was a connection between her family and how concerned they were with appearances affecting her in the club. She still had a lot to think through.

Lara blew out a breath as she finally got a minute to herself. The café was full. A group of bikers came in earlier, ten of them. All the tables had been full, so it had been a juggle as people finished to make sure she could get them seated together.

"Lara."

She glanced up to see her brother Keith. "What do you want?" She was tired of her family. Her mother called her at least once a week, nagging her to come to the family home for dinner. While there hadn't been any further incidents, having her brother show up wasn't completely unexpected.

"Get those bikers out of here."

Lara rolled her eyes; her brother had all but yelled the words. "They are more welcome here than you are. Please leave, or you'll force me to get the police involved."

"You won't call the police on me. Besides, with these hoodlums here, your business is going to go downhill. You're going to lose everything."

"Get over yourself." Lara looked at Eve and nodded. They'd talked about this. Eve would call the police. Lara hated doing it, but Keith wasn't giving her a choice. "I've asked you to leave." Lara kept her voice calm.

"Not with these thieves here." He raised his voice, waving his hand at the bikers.

One of the bikers stood up. Lara held her hand up, and he stopped. He had his cell phone in his hand. Great. They'd probably called Colby. "These men are worth ten of you, so let's not go there."

"You are so naive."

Lara laughed. "Keith, go home and tell Father these scare tactics are not going to work."

"What are you talking about?"

"Oh, come on. You've already threatened me by saying you're watching me. Go ahead, watch me. Then someone breaks into my duplex but takes nothing." She shook her head. Then it hit her right that she didn't have a thing to be afraid of. What she did in her private life was private. If people couldn't handle that, it wasn't her problem. A weight lifted off her shoulders.

"It's for your own good. You're dating a guy who runs a leather store."

"I am. Colby is his name. He's a good man and runs a legitimate business."

"You need to listen to me."

"No, I don't." Lara turned as her brother threw out his

hands. Pain exploded over her cheek.

"That's assault," a male voice said as the bikers all rose to their feet. Another one pulled his cell out.

"Do not call him," Lara said to the bikers as she held her hand up to them. She didn't want them getting into trouble. She glared at her brother.

"Oh my God. Lara, it was an accident. I swear it was."

"Get out, Keith, and don't come back. Ever." The throbbing in her cheek made her head hurt. Her brother turned and high-tailed it out of the café. Officer Wolfe held the door open.

"Outside," Logan said to Keith, then he spoke to Lara. "You need some ice."

"Why are you always the one to answer the call?" she asked.

"Just lucky." He shrugged and led her to an empty chair.

"Here's some ice," Eve said, handing Lara ice wrapped in a towel.

"Thanks."

"I'll take care of the customers," Eve said and bustled away.

Lara put the ice to her cheek and winced.

"You're going to have one hell of a bruise," Logan said, pulling out his notebook. "Want to tell me what happened?"

Lara told Logan, with the bikers confirming her report as did several of the customers who came up to make sure she was okay. They'd just finished up when Colby came flying into the café.

She let out a groan and glared at the bikers.

"It wasn't me," Logan said, standing. Turning to Lara, he said, "If you want to press charges, let me know."

"Thanks."

Logan passed Colby and said something too soft for Lara to hear. Colby's shoulders lost some of their tension as he walked toward her. He stopped and clapped a couple of the bikers on the shoulder, then he was in front of her.

"Are you okay?"

"The best I can be at the moment."

Colby lifted his hand and ran his palm over her hair. "How bad?"

"It was an accident." She did believe that. Her brother had been truly horrified.

"You're not listening. How bad?" He tapped her hand holding the ice to her cheek.

Lara lowered her hand. Colby's eyes turned glacial.

"It's red, but at least the ice is helping, so it's not swelling much. Keep the ice on for another ten minutes," he said, his voice controlled.

"I will. You didn't need to rush over here."

"I will always come when you need me." He looked at the bikers and inclined his head.

Colby's cell rang. He let out a sigh and answered. "Yes, okay Kase, I'll be right there." He glanced at her, indecision in his gaze.

"Go," Lara said. "Kase needs you."

"Call me when you're ready to leave for the day. No excuses," he said when she opened her mouth. "I want to make sure you get home okay."

"Yes." Lara dropped her voice. "Sir."

Colby's eyes flared with passion. "Behave." He touched her nose before turning and walking out of the café with the bikers following him.

* * * *

Colby stepped outside the café and took a deep breath.

174

"Don't do anything rash, Colby," Logan said from where he lounged against his vehicle.

"Glad you're still here. Her brother is at my shop creating trouble."

Logan straightened. "Let's go. I'm getting sick of him."

"You know if you arrest him, he'll be out on bail within hours," Colby said as they power-walked down the street to his shop.

"I know, but there have to be consequences to his actions. It might have been an accident that he hit Lara, but I'm getting tired of him harassing her."

"You and me both." Colby pushed open the door to his shop to see Lara's brother Keith arguing with Kase.

"Oh good," Keith said when he saw Colby and Logan. "This man accused me of stealing."

"I did no such thing," Kase said.

"Take a break, Kase," Colby said to the man. Kase was a good guy, but Keith calling Kase a liar was a hot spot. Kase spent time in juvie for a crime he didn't commit.

"Sure, boss." Kase walked away into the small employee area they had.

Colby turned to Keith. "Look, I don't care if you don't like me, what I sell, or the people I sell to. But leave Lara and my employees the hell alone."

"She's my sister."

"She's my girlfriend." What a mundane name for what he felt for Lara. She was so much more. How much? Colby's heart warmed at the thought, but this wasn't the time. He pushed it into a small corner of his heart to figure out later. Right now, he had business to take care of.

"Family first."

Colby rolled his eyes.

"I want that employee fired," Keith said.

"Not going to happen." Colby looked at Logan. "Give me a minute." Colby pulled out his phone and found what he wanted. "Logan." Colby handed him his phone.

Logan pressed the play button and watched the vid, his eyes widening. Just as he looked at Keith, two more police officers walked into Colby's shop. "I called for backup from outside the café," Logan said as he handed Colby his phone back.

"Mr. Meyer, based on evidence, I need to search you," Logan said.

"Absolutely not. Especially not without my lawyer," Keith said, crossing his arms over his chest. "I want my lawyer."

"Very well." Logan let out a sigh. "Mr. Meyer, you are being arrested on suspicion of theft. You have a right to an attorney, which you have requested." Logan read him the rest of his rights.

Colby couldn't believe this, but he understood Logan had to act within the law. Keith was handcuffed and led away, spouting threats about how he'd have everyone's jobs before this was through.

"I'll need a copy of that security tape," Logan told him.

"Come into my office, and I'll email it to you while you're watching so no one can claim it was doctored."

"When did you put in the cameras?" Logan asked as they walked back to the office.

"A few weeks ago, not because there was a problem. It just made sense at the time. Now, I'm glad I did it." Colby brought up the file on his computer, copied it, and sent it in an email to Logan.

"I am too." They walked back out to the front of the store. Several of the bikers from the café were there, shopping. "You do realize he'll be out on bail in a few hours," Logan said.

"Yeah. But at least maybe they'll realize I'm not going to be an easy target." Colby drew his hand over his face. "I'm more worried about Lara."

"Talk with her. I know you grew up here, as I did, but we ran in different circles. I know the Meyer family. They think they're better than everyone else," Logan said.

"Lara isn't like that." Colby frowned.

"I know." Logan waved his hand in the air. "Lara has always bucked the family, and they don't like it."

Colby nodded and Logan left. It was barely two in the afternoon, but Colby wanted to go back over to the café. Issac walked into the shop. "What are you doing here?"

"Kase called. Go take care of your lady; we can handle the shop and close up tonight," Issac said.

Colby didn't hesitate. "Thanks. You both deserve bonuses this month." He grabbed his jacket and keys.

Eve was fussing over Lara when he walked back into the café. Now that the lunch rush was done, there were only a few people still in the café.

"How's the cheek?" Colby asked.

"It hurts," Lara said, her voice not quite steady.

"Take her home, Colby. I can clean up and close up," Eve said.

"But—"

"Thank you, Eve." Colby wasn't going to let Lara protest. He pulled her to her feet. "Let's get your things." He was surprised when she didn't argue, and that told him just how much she was hurting.

Colby got Lara home, had her take two aspirin, and lie down. He sat with her until her eyes closed and her breathing evened out. Her cheek was going to be one big bruise by tomorrow.

Anger hit his blood stream. He left her bedroom and called Kase and asked him if, once they closed the shop, he'd drive his bike over to Lara's. Issac could pick Kase up and take him back to the shop for his car. They both told him yes. He was probably overstepping boundaries, but he called Jordan.

"Hey, Colby, what can I do for you?"

"I'm not sure." Colby rubbed his neck.

"What's happened?"

Colby outlined what happened at the café and at his shop.

"Well, the best I can do is try and get a restraining order, especially for the café after he hit Lara. Accident or not, it shows he's out of control."

"I'll talk with Lara. I don't like what her family is doing."

"I don't either, but they're pretty much staying within the law."

"Thanks." Colby hung up. There was a soft knock on the front door. He got up, and when he looked out, he smiled. He opened the door. "Hi, Tammy."

"Colby. I was surprised to see Lara home this early."

Colby gestured for her to enter. Once she was seated on the sofa, he sat down and took her hand. "Lara's sleeping." He kept his voice low.

"Is she sick?"

Colby wanted to tell her yes, but he wouldn't lie. "No. Keith came to the café, there was an accident, and he hit Lara."

Aunt Tammy's hand covered her mouth. "Accident, my ass," she muttered.

"That's how I feel, but Lara said it was an accident and

refused to press charges."

"I should call that brother of mine and give him a piece of my mind."

A grin tilted Colby's lips. "You know Lara wouldn't want that."

"She's a lot more forgiving than I am. And tenderhearted too."

"Tell me more," Colby said, letting himself relax against the sofa.

"It will be my pleasure."

Chapter 13

The next evening, Lara groaned. No matter what she did, she couldn't hide the bruise on her cheek completely. Maybe she should cancel tonight at the club. She wasn't catering tonight.

But if she canceled, she would be giving in to her family and letting Colby down, which she wasn't about to do. She knew it was an accident, but if Keith had left when she told him, her cheek wouldn't be black and blue.

She didn't understand what her family had against the bikers or the leather shop or her café. Their excuses were appearances and reflection on the family name. They were the ones causing trouble, not her. Lara let out a sigh. With a grimace, she left the bathroom and looked at the outfit on her bed. Her standard boy shorts, but she'd chosen a lacy bra tonight.

Her doorbell rang. She slipped on a coat and looked out to see Colby standing there. She pulled open the door. "Hi." She smiled and then immediately grimaced.

"It still hurts." Colby fingers skimmed her bruised check.

"Only when I smile." It was true. The pain was gone. She'd iced it off and on today to keep the swelling down.

"Don't joke."

"I'm fine." She captured his fingers as they slid down her face and brought them up and caressed them with her lips. Desire flared in Colby's eyes.

"I'm glad you're not catering tonight."

"Me too." She paused. "I'm so glad you're in my life." She released his hand and picked up her purse. "I'm ready."

At the club, Ralph raised an eyebrow when they checked in but didn't say anything. When they reached the ladies' room, Lara took Colby's hand. "When you get off work tonight, you're mine."

"Isn't that my line?"

She grinned.

Colby stilled. "Lara, what are you up to?"

She put her hand on his shoulder. "See you inside the club." Rising on her toes, she brushed a kiss over his lips, then slipped into the ladies' room.

Letting out a breath, Lara went to a locker and put her purse and the jacket in it. She turned to the mirror. She gathered her hair up and secured it. She wasn't sure what the night would bring. Her nipples tightened in anticipation.

Colby's eyes had flared when she told him he was hers. She'd figured it was obvious. Taking a breath, she turned and left the bathroom. Even though she told Colby she'd meet him inside the club, she half expected him to be here waiting for her.

"Excuse me, Ms. Lara." Ralph's voice was soft.

"Yes, Ralph." She turned her head and saw him standing right beyond the doorway.

"Is everything okay with you and Dom Colby?" His gaze went to her cheek before returning to meet hers.

"Thank you, Ralph. All is fine. This"—she waved her hand at her cheek—"Was done by someone else."

"I hope Dom Colby made him pay."

"He did." Lara smiled. She'd heard all about Keith's arrest. Of course, he was released right away, but maybe her family would realize Colby wasn't going to put up with their bullshit. Neither was she. Not anymore.

"Have a good evening," Ralph said, turning as another couple walked into the club.

Warmed by the concern Ralph had shown, Lara walked into the club. The music was already going, and the beat made her start rocking her head. She glanced around and saw Colby talking with Max. She knew Colby was on duty from eight to ten tonight.

She slowly walked across the floor to where the two men stood near the bar. The next thing she knew, Regina, Hannah, and Emily surrounded her. The club was eerily quiet even with the music playing.

Lara glanced at the women, then around the club where other Doms stared at Colby.

"You need to talk to Master Max," Regina said.

"Yes. He'll help you," Hannah said.

"Master Max will keep you safe," Emily commented.

"What?" Lara looked over Regina's shoulder to see the Doms moving toward Colby.

"I can't believe Sir Colby hit you," Hannah said.

Lara placed her hand on her cheek. Oh goodness. They were all protecting her. Her heart melted. "It's okay."

"No, it's not." Emily put her hands on her hips. "He shouldn't have hit you."

Lara blew out a breath. "He didn't. Sir Colby would never raise his hand to me or any woman. It was someone else." So this was what it was like to have a family that cared. Her heart stuttered.

The women relaxed around her, and Lara used their relief to slip between them and over to Colby. She cuddled right up to him, and his eyes widened.

"Master Max," Lara said. "Would you please make an

announcement for me?"

"What do you want me to say?" Max asked.

"Tell everyone Colby didn't hit me." She glanced over her shoulder at the Doms.

Colby's arms encircled her waist.

"I have a better idea." Max leaned around the bar and the music died. "Logan," he called, and he walked over. The crowed murmured. "Quiet." Max's voice carried throughout the club, and instantly there was silent. "Logan, if you would please."

Lara wondered what was going on. But she stayed silent.

"Everyone settle down," Logan said. "The bruise on Lara's face was caused by her brother, not Colby. Colby would never raise his hand to a woman. The man responsible was arrested and charges were filed. So there's no need to for all this posturing."

The Doms shook their heads and began to move away, the music started back up. "Thank you, Sir Logan," Lara said. "I didn't want anyone in the club to think Colby did it."

"Glad to help." Logan walked away.

"Excuse me," Max said and left.

"Sweetheart, you didn't need to do that," Colby said.

"Of course I did. Everyone thought I was covering for you. They don't know me well enough to know I won't stand for a man who hits a woman. Besides, this way everyone knows at the same time."

Colby shook his head. "Nice bra." His fingers traced the thin strap.

"I believe it's appropriate club wear, Sir." She went up on her toes. "Later, I'll let you peel it off me."

His eyes flared with passion. "It's going to be a long

shift tonight. Stay in the green area, and I'll come and get you when I'm done."

"Yes, Sir. I only want you."

Colby escorted her over to the green area. Hannah smiled and patted the seat next to her. "Until later," Colby said, kissing her hard before walking away.

"Now tell us how you captured Colby's heart?" Hannah asked.

* * * *

Colby strolled around the club with a lightness he hadn't expected. After Logan's explanation, everyone had gone back to their business. The club really was a family.

He hadn't expected them to react that way to the bruise on Lara's cheek Then again, the Doms and subs were all protective. He was glad too.

Colby shifted. When Lara had told him he could peel the bra off her body later, his dick went from semi-hard to a full on erection at her words. While he wasn't sure if she meant here in the club or at home, it didn't matter.

Luckily his shift went fairly quickly. He kept glancing over at Lara talking with the subs in the green area. She looked very relaxed and happy. It did his heart good to see it. She belonged here, and maybe she was starting to feel that way as well.

* * * *

When his shift was almost over, Colby glanced over to the green area. Jordan had had an emergency, and Max needed someone to cover the midnight to two shift. Colby told him he'd stay. In between, he and Lara had taken in a couple of scenes.

She was doing better with him touching her in the club. While she reacted when he started to play with her breasts and nipples, she wasn't tense, nor did she pull away. When he told her he needed to stay, she offered to stay too. No sense in him trying to figure out how to get home since they came in her car.

She was curled up in one of the overstuffed chairs, half asleep. She'd had a rough couple of days. He was pretty sure her cheek still hurt.

"Take her home," Max said.

"But..."

"I can handle this. Logan is hanging out until closing time, so we've got this."

"Thanks." Colby walked into the green area. "Night, Hannah." She'd been sitting with Lara for the last hour.

"Night, Sir Colby." Hannah stood up and walked over to Logan.

"Lara?" Colby leaned down and brushed a kiss over her lips.

"Hmmm."

"Come on, honey. Time to go home." Colby picked her up.

"I can walk," she said, her voice drowsy.

"I'm sure you can." He carried her into the ladies' room and had her open her locker to retrieve her things. When he walked out, Hannah was standing there with a blanket. She draped it over Lara.

"Bless you, Hannah." Colby nodded to Ralph as he left.

Thank goodness for remote entry. He maneuvered the door open and set Lara onto the passenger seat. After making sure she was buckled in, he adjusted the blanket over her.

Colby shivered as he climbed in. It might be the beginning of May, but the nights in the Pacific Northwest were still chilly. He started the car, and before they made it to the main road, heat began filling the vehicle.

Lara snuggled into the blanket. She let out a sigh.

She'd trusted him enough to let go. To allow him to play with her breasts in the club. Yeah, they'd done it before, but tonight was different. No tensing up, no worry about who saw them. She'd been relaxed and leaned into his touch. It made the Dom in him proud. He drove to his place and carried her into his bedroom. The shorts were okay, but that bra had to go so she'd be comfortable. He unhooked it and drew the covers over her. She snuggled right under them.

She looked so good in his bed. He wanted her to stay there forever. The thought didn't scare him. Lara had wormed her way into his heart, and he was going keep her there. He grinned as he made his way into the bathroom. After a quick, hot shower, he slid between the covers with her, gathered her into his arms, and closed his eyes.

* * * *

Lara's cell phone rang for the fourth time as Colby drove to her home. "I guess I better get it," she said.

"I don't think your mother is going to stop until you do," Colby commented. He understood why she was avoiding the call, but it was apparent her mother wasn't going to give up.

"Hey, Mom," Lara said. She stiffened and looked over at Colby. "There is nothing to discuss." A pause. "I'm sorry, but this is my life." Her fingers tightened around the phone. "Sorry you can't deal with it, but it's my life, and I'll live it the way I choose. I am an adult."

Lara ended the call and powered off her phone before tossing it in her bag.

"That didn't sound like a very good discussion."

She snorted. "There was no discussion. I'm supposed to toe the line. Well, guess what? I'm not." She folded her arms over her chest.

"I don't understand your family." He held his hand out and was pleased when she placed hers in his. His fingers closed over hers. "Your aunt isn't like your parents and brothers are."

"Aunt Tammy has always been my rock. She's always supported me."

"Why not your mother?" He really wanted to understand more about her family.

Lara let out a sigh. "My mother follows whatever my father says. She's one of those women who was raised to obey her husband."

"I see." He did. There were a lot of women in his neighborhood that were like that. Over the years, he'd tried to make sure they understood times were changing and got some counselors in to help them.

"Yeah." She squeezed his hand. "I don't believe in the obey part of the marriage vows. I refused to speak them."

"Except in our bedroom, right?" he grinned.

"Only with you." Lara answered without hesitation, making the Dom in him proud as hell.

"Still, I bet your family was upset when you wouldn't say those words."

"They were, and you know what? I don't care anymore."

The finality in her voice made him proud. Lara was a strong woman, much stronger than she realized. When Colby pulled up to her house, there was a man pacing outside her home on the sidewalk.

"Damn," she muttered.

"Who is he?" Colby asked.

"My ex." Lara opened the door and stepped out before Colby could stop her. He hopped out and hurried to her side.

"What do you want, Walter?"

"I—" Her ex broke off when Colby joined them. "What is he doing here?" His voice rose as he glared at Colby.

"It's none of your business. Go home." Lara kept her tone steady, but Colby could hear the frustration in it.

"It is my business; you're my wife."

"Ex-wife and I have been for almost four years."

"Your parents—"

"I don't care what my parents want. Get that through your head. We're divorced. We're not getting back together. I've moved on, Walter, it's time you did too." Lara tilted her head up. "Let's go inside, Colby."

Colby kept his arm around Lara's waist and guided her past Walter. There was movement to his right, and suddenly, Lara spun in his hold.

"Don't you fucking touch me." She pressed her back against Colby's chest.

"I only..."

Colby stepped around Lara. "You need to leave, now." He was holding on to his temper by a thread, but that was only because Lara was standing behind him.

Walter hastily stepped back, turned, and briskly walked away. Colby turned back to Lara. "Are you okay?"

"Yes." She let out a sigh. "Why can't my family get it into their heads I am not going to get back with Walter, nor am I going to fall in line with any of their plans."

"Stubbornness."

"Well, I can be stubborn too. Plus, I have better friends."

"That you do." Colby made a mental note to let Logan know about what happened today with her ex.

Chapter 14

Lara waved as the bikers left the café, and she emptied the tip jar. They tipped so well. She was happy. The last two weeks had flown. The café was constantly busy from nine until two.

She'd hired a young man who would cover Saturday afternoons with Megan while Lara got everything ready for the catering gig at the club. Lara had talked with Max about having someone come pick up the hot boxes rather than her bringing them out that night. It was a lot of work for her to do that, in addition to having to load and unload them in her car.

Max had given her one better. He bought two hot boxes for the club and a half-dozen insulated thermal bags. She could use the thermal bags to put the pans in and take to the club. They'd stay warm, and the hot boxes would stay at the club.

Plus, once she set up, she would have help when she needed it. Hannah was a godsend. This way if she and Colby wanted to play, they could.

Less traveling for her, less mess and everything. She was excited about this new venture. Not only catering the club, but she'd talked with Mr. Torrino, and he was thrilled to sell the ice cream shop to her so she could expand her café.

Lara had met with her accountant this morning. She'd

need a new loan, but it was more than doable, and the accountant would accompany Lara to the bank to get the loan. Not her father's bank, this time. She wanted out from under her father. So she mentioned to her accountant that she was thinking about combining both loans into one.

She agreed it made sense, but she suggested adding some extra capital. Lara made a note to call Zeke about the remodel. He'd taken a cursory look around the ice cream shop and her café to give her an idea of what could be done. They needed to make solid plans once she had the loan.

Lara was feeling optimistic, not only about her business but about her life. She and Colby spent most of their free time together. Either at her house or his apartment. They'd had dinners with his mom and Aunt Tammy, who enjoyed talking with each other and had more in common than Lara thought they would. Life was good.

With a sigh, Lara finished cleaning up the café, making sure everything was ready for tomorrow morning. Then she grabbed her purse, set the alarm on the café, and closed the back door, double-checking it was locked. She dropped her keys in her purse. It had been a long day. An SUV pulled up. Lara hesitated. Her brothers climbed out.

"I have nothing to say to either of you," she said.

"That's fine," Keith said, taking her right arm and Scott taking her left.

"What are you doing?" For the first time in her life, she feared her brothers.

"Getting you in the car." Keith and Scott pulled her toward the SUV.

"No." Lara struggled with them.

"Come on, Lara," Scott said softly. "Mom and Dad just want to talk with you."

"Hell, no." She almost got her arm loose from Scott,

when Keith twisted her right arm behind her back.

"You have to do things the hard way, don't you?" Something slipped over her wrist as Scott pulled her left arm behind her. Her wrists were secured behind her back.

Lara opened her mouth, and Keith clamped his hand over her face. "No yelling, no screaming." As much as she fought and thrashed, they were still able to get her into the SUV.

"This is kidnapping," she said as Keith pulled out from behind her café.

"They just want to talk," Scott said.

Lara struggled in her seat. "I politely refused. Don't think I won't press charges. I'm done." She was. This was the final straw. She wasn't putting up with her family anymore. It was time they got the message, and if it took a court battle, so be it. When they got to the family home, Keith pulled in back.

Lara allowed them to pull her out of the car and into the house. Once she was out of the cuffs, she'd leave. There was no way she'd allow them to keep her confined in this house. Her parents and Walter were waiting. Great. Walter was the last thing she needed.

"You tied her up?" Walter's voice held outrage.

"She fought us," Keith said.

"Get them off," Walter ordered.

Keith glared at Walter, but soon her hands were free. Lara rubbed her wrists. Thank goodness she had her purse across her body.

"I'm sorry, Lara; we just wanted to talk to you," Walter said.

"I said no." She marched toward the door. "I'm done talking."

Her father grabbed her arm. "You have to stop seeing

that man."

"*That man*, as you call him, has a name. Colby. He's a better man than all of you. You need to let me go. I'm already charging those two idiots"—she waved her free hand at her brothers—"with kidnapping, so unless you want to be charged as an accessory…" Her father let her go, and her fingers curled around the doorknob.

"Lara, please." Her mother's soft voice stopped her. "We're just trying to stop you from making a mistake."

"No." Lara turned. "You're trying to control my life. I'm done. Expect the police." This time she was able to open the door and leave. They didn't try and stop her. She could hear arguing, Walter, her father, and her two brothers.

Two blocks from the house, Lara realized she couldn't walk home. She pulled out her cell. Colby? No, she wouldn't pull him away from his business for this. If he got angry with her for it, so be it. This was her choice. Her fingers curled around the small business card she'd thrown in there weeks ago. Time to stand up for herself against her family.

"Officer Wolfe."

"Hi, Officer Wolfe, this is Lara Meyer."

"Is there something wrong?"

Lara heard the alert in his voice. "Yes." Tears welled in her eyes. "I'm at the corner of Fifteenth and Paulson; I need to report a kidnapping."

"Colby?"

"No, me." This time, there was no stopping the tears as fear overwhelmed her. She'd never been truly afraid of her family until now. What if her family came after Colby? "I need to warn Colby."

"I'll take care of it. I have a car on the way to your location right now. Stay on the phone with me."

"Okay." Lara kept an eye out for her family as the tears continued to fall. She normally wasn't this emotional, but damn it. After being on a high about her life, now it was falling apart. She heard Logan speaking but not the words.

"Ms. Meyer."

Lara let out a cry and spun around.

"Lara," Logan yelled.

"It's okay, Logan. The officers you sent are here." She hadn't even heard them arrive. "I'm hanging up now." She wiped the tears away.

"Ms. Meyer, I'm Officer Adams, and this is Officer Harris." He gestured to the female officer.

"Thank you for getting here so fast."

"Let's get you to the station and take your statement." They guided her to the car. While she had to sit in back, Lara felt safe, and she could finally breathe.

When they reached the police station, the officers guided her inside. Colby was pacing by Logan's desk. Colby's gaze clashed with hers. The relief in his eyes made the tears well up again. She loved this man so much.

In an instant, Colby folded her into his arms. "Sweetheart, I'm here."

She put her arms around his waist and snuggled up to him. Now she felt totally safe. Colby wouldn't let anything happen to her. While, intellectually, she knew she could stand on her own two feet, being in Colby's arms felt right.

"Why don't we take this to the conference room," Logan said.

"Sure," Colby said. He kept her close to his side and even inside the conference room, he pushed his chair close to hers and took her hand.

"Lara, tell me what happened," Logan said.

Lara told him about how she left her business, and her

brothers were there; they forced her into the SUV and cuffed her hands behind her back. Colby lifted her arm, and there were red marks on her wrist.

"Oh." She lifted her other arm; there were marks there as well.

"Let me go get a camera to document those marks." Logan left and returned. Her wrists were photographed, and she continued with her story up until the point where she called Logan.

"So we have your brothers for kidnapping, and your parents and ex-husband as accessories."

"Yes." Lara froze. "Aunt Tammy. Oh my God, Colby. What if they go after Aunt Tammy?" Her voice rose.

"It's okay." Colby rubbed her shoulder. "I sent a couple of the guys over to watch her place when Logan called me and told me you were in trouble."

Lara slumped in her chair. "Thank you."

"Do you think your family will go after your aunt?" Logan asked.

"At this point, who knows what they'll do. I never thought they'd try to kidnap me. This is really going to drag their names through the mud."

"I wouldn't worry about them," Colby said.

"Now what?" Lara asked.

"You're willing to press charges, right?" Logan asked.

"What will happen?" Lara didn't want to let her brothers get away with what they did, yet... What? They didn't have to kidnap her.

"I arrest them, all of them," Logan said.

"And after that?"

"They'll be processed, and the DA's office gets involved to see if they want to prosecute or not."

"My father has friends in the DA's office," Lara

muttered.

"Can we get our own prosecuting attorney?" Colby asked.

"Not for the criminal case. You can pursue a suit in civil court in addition to the criminal case, and you could ask for damages. But either way, you'll need discuss that with your attorney," Logan said.

"I'll take care of it." Colby stood and pulled out his phone as he walked out the door.

"How soon will they be out on bail?" she asked Logan.

"Depends on the judge at their arraignment once you press charges. But you should talk to a lawyer about pursuing a civil case. In any event, you definitely want to retain counsel to help you through the criminal and civil process. This is second degree kidnapping, a class B felony. Your brothers and parents are in some serious trouble."

"Jordan and Crystal are on their way," Colby said, reentering the room.

"I'll escort them in here so you can talk. Once you make a decision, I'll take it from there." Logan stood. "If you need anything, let me know."

Lara crossed her arms over her stomach.

"I need to hold you." Colby's husky tone made Lara shiver.

"I need that too." She stood, and Colby pulled her onto his lap, her legs over the arm of the chair. Colby buried his face in her neck. "They hurt you."

"I won't say they didn't." Not only were her wrists sore, but her heart was bloodied and bruised.

"I'm sorry," she said softly.

"For what, sweetheart?"

"I didn't call you."

His arms tightened around her. "While I would have

preferred you did, I understand why you called Logan. You were scared, and the police were necessary, just in case."

"That was part of it." She tilted her head back and gazed up at him. "I didn't want you to get hurt if my family did come after me."

"Never again, sweetheart." He brushed a soft kiss over her forehead.

They sat there in silence until Jordan and Crystal walked in. Lara straightened, and Colby tightened his hold, then released her. She slid off his lap and took her seat.

"Logan gave the rundown version; I'd like to hear from you," Jordan said, taking a seat across from Lara with Crystal by his side.

"Are you okay, Lara?" Crystal asked.

"As best as I can be." She let out a sigh. Colby took her hand in his as she told the story again. When she finished, Jordan had a grim look on his face, and Crystal was frowning.

"And I thought my family was a mess," Crystal muttered.

"Are you willing to press charges?" Jordan asked.

Colby squeezed her hand.

"What will happen, Jordan?" Lara asked.

"Once you press charges, they'll be arrested, booked, and held in jail until they are arraigned and bail is set. If they don't post bail, they'll be held in jail until the trial. Your story meets the criteria for second degree kidnapping under the Washington State code for your brothers and accessories to same for your parents and ex. Kidnapping is a serious felony and carries significant jail time. To save the cost of a trial, the DA might offer them a deal, but there is likely going to be jail time in any event. I can speak to the DA and look out for your interests in the criminal case, and we can decide later if you want to pursue a civil case.

"And how long will all of this take?" Lara didn't want this to drag on for years.

"Depends. Once you agree to press charges, Logan has enough evidence for an arrest warrant. Your parents' and brothers' lawyer or lawyers will do everything they can to delay and make life difficult for everyone, but your brothers were not careful. They were picked up on security cameras, and those videos and the marks on your arms make this a pretty much open and shut case. If we get a no-nonsense judge, this could move relatively quickly."

"What videos?" She stared at Jordan.

Jordan looked at Colby.

"I may have had someone check the camera feeds in the alley from other businesses. You're not the only one with them." He met her gaze. That was Colby, see a problem and find a solution.

Lara closed her eyes. If she didn't do this, they would never stop. If she did, it would destroy what little relationship she had with her family. No question, that relationship was toxic. It was time to cut ties.

"I'll press charges against my brothers and ex. I'd like to leave my parents out of it with a warning."

Jordan nodded, stood up and called Logan in.

* * * *

Three weeks later, Lara was still waiting for the other shoe to drop. She still worried if she'd done the right thing or not. Colby and Aunt Tammy both assured her she had. The café was bustling as always, so it helped her keep her mind off of everything.

As she guessed, her brothers and ex were out on bail the day after the arraignment. She hadn't pressed charges against her parents. She couldn't bring herself to do it. But

197

her brothers and ex weren't going to stop. Jordan was in contact with her as the family lawyer was trying to work plea deal.

Jordan kept her informed and advised her. So far what the family lawyer was asking for was a joke, and she wasn't going to let them get off with a slap on the wrist. The DA had also made it clear that whatever deal was struck, her brothers and ex were definitely going to do some serious jail time, but the DA was open to less than the ten year maximum.

Lara smiled at the bikers, who were sitting at a table in the café. They were here later than normal, but she suspected Colby had something to do with that.

"Do you guys need refills on anything?" she asked.

"No, thank you. We're good."

"Okay." Lara turned away from them as someone walked into the café. She stiffened. "Get out, Walter."

Walter held his hand out in front of him. "Hear me out, Lara." He glanced at the bikers behind her. "You need to drop the charges against me and your brothers."

"Not going to happen."

"If you don't, I'll go to the press about you and your boy toy. I know what you've been up to."

"Are you threatening me?"

The bikers stood, walked over, and formed a protective half moon around Lara, who was grateful for their presence.

"You'll regret this," Walter sneered.

"I doubt it."

Walter turned and stormed out.

"Thank you," Lara turned to the bikers.

"He threatened you," one of the bikers said.

"Bear is right," another said.

"I'm fine." She waved them back to their seats and

made her way behind the counter. She wasn't all right. What did her ex know? How would that affect her business and Colby's?

She glanced at the bikers. No phones. She should call Colby, but he'd told her he had a meeting today with a major store who wanted him to make some specialized items for them. She'd tell him about this later. He had to trust her to do what was right for her. With a sigh, she picked up the phone and called Jordan to let him know what had happened.

Jordan said he'd draw up paperwork for no-contact orders. It should have been done at the arraignment, Jordan wasn't sure how it was overlooked, and told her he'd get back to her once he'd talked with a judge. They might be able to do this without a formal hearing. Lara hung up and sighed. Her family was making this difficult, but what else did she expect?

The bikers stayed until she closed up, and then she noticed Bear was keeping watch until she drove away. The bikers were good guys and didn't deserve to be treated like dirt.

Lara hardened her heart against her family. No more feeling sorry for them. They caused this chaos not her. Unfortunately, she was also paying the price for it. She had some tough decisions to make.

* * * *

"Want to tell me what's bothering you?" Colby said after dinner at Lara's house.

"Nothing." Lara flittered around the kitchen. Why was she hesitating in telling him what happened today?

"Bull." Colby placed his hands on her shoulders. "I can't help you if you won't talk to me."

She needed to tell him, or she'd betray his trust in her.

199

"My ex came by the café today."

"He what!" Colby whirled away from Lara as his fingers curled into fists. "Why the hell didn't you tell me this sooner?"

"Because I knew it would upset you."

"And you're not upset?" He stared at her.

"I am."

"What did he say?"

"Colby, this is what I was worried about. You getting all angry over Walter showing up."

Colby's stared at her. "Of course, I'm angry. That man was part of your kidnapping."

"He didn't kidnap me, my brothers did."

Colby took a deep breath. "He was an accessory, and you agreed to the charges. Here's what we're going to do. We are going to go sit down, and you are going to tell me exactly what happened." His voice was deep. His Dom side was coming out. He would protect her.

Lara sighed, but he was right. He needed to know.

Colby guided her to the sofa and tugged her down. "Tell me."

She poured out the story, and Colby made a mental note to give Bear and his friends not only his thanks but a discount at the shop. When Lara was done, Colby's temper hadn't cooled. The ex tried to blackmail her. Another nail in the coffin.

He pulled out his cell, put it on speaker, and dialed.

"What's up, Colby?" Jordan's voice came through the speaker.

"What are you doing about Lara's ex?" Colby's voice was demanding answers.

"I've got a meeting with a judge tomorrow about a no-contact order."

"What about the blackmail?"

"What? Lara didn't tell me about blackmail. Give me the details."

Colby glared at her before he laid out that her ex had threatened to go to the press about something he had on Colby. The only thing Colby could think of was the club.

"Well, after Damon and Tessa, everyone knows about the club anyhow," Jordan said.

"I don't want any backlash to anyone at the club, let alone any of you," Lara said.

"All I can say is that we'll be fine. Do you want to add to the charges already filed against your ex? It will be your word against his since there are no witnesses," Jordan said.

"Oh but there are," Colby said. "Bear and his men were in the café. They heard everything."

"Well, that changes things. The ball is in your court, Lara," Jordan said.

"Can I think about it?"

"Sure. Give me a call tomorrow morning, early. I'll be talking to the judge at ten about no-contact orders, so that's another ball in our corner." The line went dead.

"You should press charges," Colby said.

"I know, but I don't want anyone else affected by my stupid family." She rubbed her forehead. "I don't want anything to blow back on the club. I'm thinking about more than just me and you."

"Well, let's just take care of that, too." Colby grinned and dialed another number, putting his phone on speaker. "Wicked Sanctuary, Max speaking."

Lara's eyes widened.

"Max, it's Colby." He quickly outlined what had happened and Lara's concerns.

"Go after the bastard," Max said. "I'm sure everyone

knows about the club by now. We'll be fine. After Damon and Tessa's press conference, membership actually went up."

"Thanks, Max." Colby hit the end button and looked at Lara. "Does that help?"

"Yes, but honestly, I need to talk to Aunt Tammy; this could affect her as well."

"Then let's talk to her." No matter what Lara tried to put in his way, Colby was going to get her to press blackmail charges against her ex, even if she dropped them later or they pleaded out. But he was glad she'd talked to Jordan about a restraining order.

Next door, Lara, at Colby's insistence, laid out what had happened.

"Walter did what?" Aunt Tammy hit the table with her hand before she stood up and crossed the room and picked up her landline phone.

"Aunt Tammy?" Lara asked.

Tammy waved her hand. Colby watched Tammy's face; she was mad. Spitting mad, as Colby's mother would say.

"Lawrence, enough is enough."

Lara jumped up from the table, but her aunt put her hand up, and Lara stopped in her tracks.

"I mean it, Lawrence. I've had enough of your shenanigans. Stop pushing Walter at Lara; he wasn't right for her. Never was. But what you're doing now is pushing the boundaries of family."

Her aunt's fingers tightened around the phone. "If that's how you feel, I can't change your mind. But I can remind you I sit on the board of the bank as the majority owner."

Lara could hear her father yelling as Aunt Tammy

hung up the phone.

"Let him chew on that," Tammy said.

"You sit on the board of the bank?" The astonishment in Lara's voice didn't surprise him, and it was good for her that the truth was coming out.

"Of course, I do." Tammy retook her seat and put her hands on the table. "My dear departed Ephraim started the bank. When he died, he made sure I was a majority owner. I let your father run it because I had no interest in running it, and he did a good job."

"But you encouraged me to go to another bank for the loan to buy the ice cream shop and expand."

"I did, because I didn't want people to think the family just gave you money. It's bad enough your father has control over the initial loan."

"Maybe not for long," Lara said, explaining she'd decided to consolidate everything under one loan, and the approval was almost done.

"Good girl," Aunt Tammy said.

"Aunt Tammy, you are a dark horse, keeping your position from us," Colby said, feeling better now than he had when Lara first told him what happened.

"I know how to play poker, young man, and don't you forget it. Now, why don't you two go home and make whoopee."

"Aunt Tammy." Lara's cheeks turned red, but Colby just laughed.

"I can't think of anything better."

Chapter 15

The next week, Lara felt like she was walking on egg shells. She hadn't heard from her ex or her brothers or her father. The silence was scary but welcome. Lara could only hope things would settle down.

She'd talked with Jordan. The judge had approved a no-contact order and gave her ex a judicial smackdown with a very stern warning that bail would be revoked if Walter stepped out of line again. In addition, the DA made it clear that they would add witness intimidation to the kidnapping charges if Walter or her brothers attempted to contact her again, so there was that. She didn't press charges against her ex for blackmail even though Colby wanted her to.

Jordan let her know the family lawyer was still trying to work a plea deal for the kidnapping charges. So far, there was nothing else worth mentioning to her, but Jordan wanted to keep her informed as things continued.

Lara glanced at the clock. "Megan, you need to get going. I don't want you to be late for your class." It was almost two, and the lunch crowd had thinned out.

"Thanks, Lara." Megan took off her apron, then got her bag from the kitchen area. "I really appreciate you allowing me time off to take my class."

Lara smiled as Megan left. Megan wanted to go back to school but needed this job, so they'd worked out a schedule.

Megan wanted to work with computers, so she started taking classes at the local college.

Lara cleaned tables and around the café. The loan officer at the bank had called her today. The loan to buy the ice cream shop was moving its way through the system, and he expected pre-approval within a week.

Good. Then she could put an offer in to Mr. Torrino and go from there. With a spring in her step, Lara stepped behind the counter as Bear and his friends came in.

"Hi, guys. The usual?"

"Perfect," Bear said.

"Yeah," came the chorus from the other three.

Lara smiled and started making their favorites. A veggie wrap, beef and bean wrap, ham and cheese sandwich, and two polish bagel dogs. She put the plates on the tray, then put together a plate of desserts.

"We didn't order dessert," Bear said when she returned with beverages.

"I know, but you guys deserve something sweet on the house." She walked away with a smile. With the amount these guys tipped, giving them dessert wasn't a big deal.

Lara was cleaning up when the door opened and two police officers walked in. "Afternoon, officers. Can I help you?"

"Good afternoon, ma'am. We've received a report of a disturbance here." The officer looked over at Bear and his friends.

"I don't know who called you, but there is no disturbance." Lara had a good idea of who made that call. Her family couldn't leave well enough alone. It also gave her confirmation that they were watching the café. She shivered. "Bear and his friends are regular customers and have never caused a problem."

"Have they intimidated you into saying that?" the blond officer asked.

"No." Lara fished her cell phone out of her pocket. "Hi, Colby, can you come down to the café, please. I'm fine. I need you." Once Colby confirmed he was on his way, she called Jordan. "Jordan, I need a lawyer at the café. Now." She nodded. "Thanks."

"My lawyer is on his way."

"You're not under arrest or anything, ma'am, but we do need to talk with the bikers."

"I didn't call for the attorney for myself, and I'd rather you wait to talk to my friends until my attorney gets here. I'm protecting their rights."

"It's okay, Lara. We'll talk with them," Bear said.

The officers approached the table. Lara noticed Bear and his friends looked wary, but they talked to the officers. Lara stood close, but not too close. As the officers turned after talking to the bikers, Colby walked in.

"Trouble?" he asked, looking at the officers.

"No. Someone—" She broke off as her brothers and ex walked into the café. She looked to the ceiling. Oh, she so didn't need them to be here.

Colby glanced over his shoulder. "I'll take care of them."

"No." Lara gripped his arm. "Officers?"

"Yes, ma'am? Sorry, we disturbed you and your patrons."

"I understand, but these three." She pointed to her brothers and ex. "I want them out of here. There is a no-contact order against all three of them, and they're out on bail on kidnapping charges."

"Oh?" the blond officer took a step toward them.

"We're family," Keith said, standing his ground.

"That doesn't matter," the first officer said as the second one stepped outside.

The bikers stood up at her words.

"They're going to kill us," Walter whispered.

"Miss Lara, thank you for the wonderful food as always," Bear said, glaring at her brothers and ex. He nodded at Colby and walked outside.

Two more police cars pulled up, along with an SUV. Logan climbed out of one of the police cars, and Jordan out of the SUV.

"Listen to us, Lara. Get rid of the bikers and your boy toy here, and all your troubles will be over," Keith said.

"Now that sounded like a threat." Logan's voice was loud and clear. He'd entered her café with the one officer. Three more stood outside.

Colby turned, keeping his body between her and her brothers, a gesture Lara appreciated, but didn't need.

"Lara?" Jordan asked.

"Do it. I'm done." She was

"Gentlemen," Logan started. "You're all under arrest for violation of a no-contact order and violating your bail conditions."

"What am I under arrest for?" Walter sputtered.

"For extortion and violation for the no-contact order." The officer grabbed Walter's wrists and cuffed him.

"It was a joke," Walter said. "Come on, Lara; you know I was only joking about exposing that you're into kink."

Silence fell on the café. Her brothers' mouths dropped open. Lara took a deep breath and held her head up. "What I do in my private life is my business, no one else's."

"Got that right," Colby muttered.

Logan gestured to her brothers.

"Fuck, we're out of here." Keith and Scott ran out of the café.

Jordan winked at her as the officers waiting outside grabbed her brothers. Lara smiled.

"Lara, I'll need you to come down and press formal charges against him for extortion," Logan said, pointing at Walter.

"I can do that."

"But..." Walter tried to speak, but the officers escorted him out before he could finish.

"Meet you at the station in an hour?" Jordan asked.

"Perfect," Colby answered.

Jordan nodded and left. Colby walked to the door and locked it, then turned back to Lara and opened his arms.

Lara ran into his embrace.

"Thank goodness that's over," Colby said.

"Do you really think so?" Lara asked. She was tired of all her family drama.

"According to Jordan, bail will be revoked for all of them. Between the kidnapping and violation of the no-contact order, and the additional blackmail charges, they're going to be in jail for a while."

Lara couldn't drum up much sympathy. They wouldn't listen to anyone. "It won't make my parents happy, but that's not my problem."

"You got that right. Grab your stuff, and we'll go down the police station and get that done."

"All right." Lara slipped out of his arms. After closing out the register and cleaning up, Lara grabbed her purse. "My car is in the alley."

Colby held out his hand, and she dropped her keys onto his palm. It was getting easier for her to let him drive her vehicle, but also her trust in him was absolute.

Two hours later, they were in her duplex. A great weight had lifted from her shoulders. Her family was dealt with as far as this last incident. She may have burned her bridges with them, but it wasn't her fault.

"Want me to call for pizza?" she asked Colby as she walked into the living room after changing into comfortable clothes.

"Come here." Colby patted the cushion next to him on the sofa. Lara tilted her head, but sat down next to him.

"My timing is going to suck." He let out a sigh. "But I can't hold back any longer. I love you."

Lara blinked. "You love me?" It wasn't that she didn't believe it, but…what?

"I do, and I have for a while now." Colby drew her into his arms.

"Why?" The word slipped out of her mouth before she could stop it.

He tilted her head back to rest on his shoulder, his green eyes serious as he gazed down at her. "You are strong, beautiful, and independent. You are a woman who knows who she is. You don't need a man to complete you, but you're willing to let me into your life. You aunt loves me, and my mother loves you."

A giggle escaped.

Colby tapped her lips in a playful gesture. "You don't mind the bikers; you aren't upset about my leather shop or motorcycle."

"Those are all part of you." Lara lifted her hand and cupped his cheek.

"You are a part of me, now." His hand slipped behind her neck. "I love you so much."

Lara's eyes filled with tears as she leaned back in Colby's embrace. "I love you too." She did. "I love your store, your motorcycle, your tenderness, and your Domness."

"Domness? I think I like that." He grinned at her.

"Of course you would." Her lips quirked. "I do love you, Colby. It was a slow progression, but you've shown me I can be strong and sexy."

"You bet." His lips captured hers.

"I picked a lousy time to say it," he said when he broke the kiss.

"It's fine." She cupped his cheek. "This is also the perfect place for us to declare our love for each other for the first time."

* * * *

Saturday night, Lara paced inside the ladies' room at the club.

"Are you sure?" Sierra asked.

"Yes." Lara was sure. She'd asked Sierra for help days ago. Tonight, she was going to be Colby's sub for his flogging demonstration. Not that he knew that. He'd already told her he'd use Regina. Not on her watch. Not anymore.

Since the blowup in the café on Tuesday and their declaration of love, she wanted to show him how much she had changed. Her family's needs were not a factor anymore. Appearances meant nothing to them; otherwise, her brothers and ex wouldn't have done what they did. Nope. She was done with all of their bullshit. She was her own woman, and she was going to do what she wanted.

Lara wanted to make Colby—and herself happy. Being his sub in the club during a flogging demonstration was another step in her freedom. She turned to the mirror. Her hair was gathered on top of her head to keep it out of the way. The purple lace baby doll outfit made her catch her breath.

The fabric was pretty thin. In fact, she could see the purple thong she was wearing underneath, though the lace cupped her breasts. Covered, but if someone looked hard enough they could see her nipples.

The neckline plunged below her breasts where a bow had been attached. The straps holding the baby doll up also had bows. But with these, one pull would allow Colby to peel the baby doll off her body.

Hell, it would probably just fall off. Taking a breath, she gathered her courage and reminded herself at the same time she was safe here and among friends. "I'm ready," she told Sierra.

"All right. Just follow behind me. We're going to knock Colby's pants off."

Lara grinned. She was ready to do this with him. She loved him. All of him. She embraced her inner vixen. Colby was hers.

* * * *

Colby set his bag on the small stage and looked at Max.

"The St. Andrew's Cross is all set for you," Max said.

"Thanks."

"Who are you using as sub tonight?"

"Regina. She doesn't mind a good flogging."

"Not Lara?"

"She's not ready."

"Are you sure about that?"

"Why would you ask that?"

Max gestured for him to turn around, and he did, just in time to see Lara step onto the stage.

Colby blinked. His eyes had to be playing tricks on him. What the hell was she wearing?

211

His gaze met hers, and he saw need and desire there. His gaze roamed over her body. She had on a purple almost see-through teddy with a matching thong. Nothing else. Her hair was pulled back.

His heart pounded. Damn, his woman was beautiful.

Yes, Lara was his woman. She had his heart and more. He'd told her he loved her and had several times more since that day in the café.

Her family was in the rear-view mirror. Aunt Tammy had put her foot down after the last stunt and called a board of directors' meeting. Apparently, there was a small, but enforceable, moral clause in the contract Lara's father signed.

Early retirement was his way out, and he took it. As for her brothers and ex, well, they were still in jail with their lawyer trying to plea them out, but the DA wasn't going to budge. The way things were progressing, she probably wouldn't be by her family or ex again for a very long time.

Lara stopped in front of him. "Sir Colby, I'm here as your sub." Her voice was soft, and she ducked her head.

Colby was stunned. "You know what this means?"

She lifted her head and took a deep breath. "Yes, Sir. I'm ready to play with you in the club. I want to feel your flogger on my ass in front of our friends and family."

Colby barely controlled the urge to pull her into his arms and kiss her silly.

"Very well." He held out his hand.

Her hand trembled slightly as she placed it in his.

He led her into the scene area, his cock pulsing with each step. "Never forget you are mine." He gave her a hard kiss before he led her to the St. Andrew's Cross. "I'm going to restrain your arms to the cross, are you okay with that?"

"Oh yes, Sir."

Her voice was breathless, and Colby's blood heated.

"I'll leave your clothing on until it's time for the flogging."

"Thank you, Sir." Her voice was soft, but that didn't stop his cock from jumping with every word she uttered. "All you have to do is undo the ties on the shoulder straps, Sir."

"Clever." Colby pulled the restraints out of his bag. "Ready sweetheart?"

"Yes, Sir."

"Safe word?"

Lara smiled. "Cookies."

He dropped a kiss on her nose and led her over to the cross. "I'll leave your ankles undone." He ran his fingers over her right arm, noting the goosebumps on her skin. "Your skin is so soft." He gently lifted her arm up and fastened the restraint, then attached it to the cross and did the same with her left arm. "Okay?"

"Yes, Sir." Her voice was soft, but steady.

"Pale skin." He dropped a kiss on her shoulder before he ran his hands down her arms, then over the sheer fabric until he reached the hem. Slipping his hands under the hem, he skimmed his fingers over her back.

A shudder went through her body. "I can't wait to see your skin pink from my flogger."

"I can't either, Sir."

Colby slipped his arms around her waist and skimmed up to cup her breasts before backing off. He undid the ties on her shoulders, and the fabric pooled around her feet.

His heart pounded as he caressed her naked back. This was his Lara.

* * * *

A shudder racked her body when Colby undid the ties.

Lara took a deep breath and closed her eyes. The cool air of the club caressed her skin. She wanted to do this. Not just for Colby but for herself. She knew he wanted to play in the club and so did she. She was ready. She loved and trusted him. The last of her fear about how others would view her melted away.

"I'm going to start with the rabbit flogger."

"Yes, Sir." They'd talked about this when playing at home. Colby would talk her through what he planned to do.

The first swat from the rabbit flogger caused her to jump, then she concentrated. The slight murmur of the voices, the swish of the flogger. Colby kept his swats to her ass. Her muscles relaxed.

Her body began to warm. That's how it was when he flogged her at home. The warming of her skin. Colby talked to the audience, but his words didn't penetrate her mind. She concentrated on the sensations flowing over her skin and the loving touch of Colby's flogger.

Colby's cool hand rubbed her ass. "How you doing?"

"Green, Sir." They'd agreed to the normal safe words except if she wanted him to stop.

"All right." Colby stepped away and began to flog her shoulders. The tension swept away from Lara.

He stopped. Again, he caressed where he flogged, talking to the crowd at the same time.

"I'm going to move up to the suede cow flogger."

"Yes, Sir." Lara took a deep breath and let it out. Her shoulders slumped. She'd been tense these past few weeks. More than she realized. The flogging was helping her relax.

The first strike of the suede flogger surprised her, and her mouth fell open. With each strike, she let her body relax into the sting on her skin. Every so often, Colby would stop and talk to her, then to the audience.

Now he was flogging her ass and the back of her thighs. The image of the subs surrounding her and the looks on the Doms faces tonight rose into her mind. Tears gathered in her eyes.

Her heart had filled with warmth and more. She'd found a community, a family. One that didn't judge her for her wants, her needs.

Tears began streaming down her face as she let go of all the emotions she'd been holding inside. The pain in her heart that her family would never understand her, the knowledge she loved Colby with all she was, and knowing her family would never accept him. Not that she cared. Not anymore. Colby was the man she wanted.

"Lara, sweetheart." Colby whispered in her ear. "That's it. Let it go." The flogger fell to the floor as he began undoing her arms. "You're with me, so there's no reason to hold back. You did so well tonight. I've got you, sweetheart."

She felt him lift her in his arms. A blanket was thrown over her. "Take care of her," Max said.

Lara's arms encircled Colby's neck as he walked away from the play area over to the aftercare area. Tears still flowing down her face. Lord, she loved this man so much it hurt.

He sat down and held her in his lap. "Lara, sweetheart. I'm so damn proud of you. You did fantastic for your first club flogging."

Lara shook her head as her tears continued to flow. "I can't stop crying." Her words were garbled. Darn it. She slid her hand up and cupped his cheek, then leaned forward and brushed a kiss over his lips.

Colby's eyes widened.

A wad of tissues was dropped into her lap. Colby

picked one up and began wiping her face.

"I'm okay," she finally said in a wobbly voice.

"Yes, you are. You are fantastic."

She tapped his cheek. "You helped me let go of all the emotion I'd been bottling up for a long time. It all came pouring out of me."

His eyes gleamed with pride. "I'm happy I could do that for you."

She pressed her palm harder against his cheek. "What you did was perfect; it allowed me a freedom I never allowed myself before."

Colby pulled her close. "That's part of what a power exchange is. Allowing each other to fly free."

"I like that."

Colby lowered his forehead to rest against hers, and they both let out a breath. They sat there for a while, then Lara shivered.

"You're cold," Colby said.

"A bit, Sir."

Colby waved Regina over and asked her to get Lara another blanket. Regina brought one over, and Colby draped it over her shoulders.

"I want to know how the scene went for you, Sir?"

"Perfect until I saw you crying. Baby, you tore my heart out with your tears."

"I'm sorry."

"Don't be. Now I know you can release your emotions that way." Colby glanced up. Lara turned her head.

Max, Jordan, Damon, Sierra, Crystal and Tessa all stood at the edge of the aftercare area. Not so close they'd interfere with Colby's aftercare, but close enough to assist if Colby or Lara needed help. Colby told them she was all right, and they slipped off to give them more privacy.

"Family," she whispered.

"Yes." Colby tightened his arms around her.

"I love you so much. You are my life." The words slipped from her lips. She'd said them before, but this time, they meant so much more.

Colby's eyes widened. He opened his mouth.

Lara placed her fingers against his lips. "Before you say anything. I want you to know that having you in my life is better than I even imagined. I needed you. You helped me get past my fears about what others might think about seeing me here."

She took a deep breath. "You've shown me so much. I've grown as a person because of you."

"I've said it before, but damn, I love you." He captured her lips with his.

Lara gave herself over to his kiss. When they broke apart, Lara laid her head down on Colby's shoulder. This is where she wanted to be. In his life, in his arms. Forever.

Epilogue

An hour later, Lara and Colby walked around the club hand in hand. Everyone smiled at them, and several of the Doms told Lara she'd done a fantastic job for her first full display.

Colby beamed. Love shone from his eyes for everyone to see, and Lara was pretty sure her love showed too.

The music stopped, and everyone turned to see Max standing at one of the stations. "Friends and family, tonight has been a wonderful night. We've played and enjoyed each other's company."

A cheer went up.

"As you know, our membership is expanding, and with that, the club is going to be expanding as well." A murmur went through the crowd.

"Does that mean you're closing for a while?" one of the Doms asked.

Max shook his head. "The club will stay open. There will be some rearranging of scenes and a few other things. Construction will start on the new portion of the club in the next few weeks. But there is another reason I'm up here tonight." Max glanced over at Sierra.

"I wonder what he's up to?" Colby asked.

"I think I might know." Lara smiled. If Max was going

to do what she thought.

"Sierra, my love." Max took a knee on the raised platform. The room stilled. "I love you with all my heart; will you become my wife and accept my collar."

"Oh. My. God. Yes." Sierra ran up to Max and threw her arms around him as he stood.

The room broke out in applause.

"You know, this means we want you to cater the bachelorette party," Crystal said walking up to Lara and Colby, with Tessa by her side.

"It would be an honor, but I think it would be much better if it was handled by a professional party planner. And I have an idea of where we can hold it." She gave the two women a grin, and they all laughed.

"What place is that?" Colby asked as the two women walked away to congratulate their friend.

Lara shook her head. "I won't spoil it, but we're going to have some girl fun."

"What kind of fun?" Colby mock-growled.

She laughed. "Nothing you won't approve of, Sir. You have my heart and my submission. For always."

"I can live with for always."

Colby kissed her, leaving no doubt in her mind that they would have a lifetime of love together.

Thank you for reading *Ravish,* the fourth book in the Wicked Sanctuary series. If you enjoyed this book, please consider leaving a review on Amazon, Goodreads, or wherever you prefer, and know that it would be greatly appreciated.

For new release information and news about Marie Tuhart, please join her newsletter.

ABOUT THE AUTHOR

Marie Tuhart lives in the beautiful Pacific Northwest. She loves to read and write, and when she's not writing, she spends time with her two dogs, Tommy and Trina, family, traveling and enjoying life.

Marie is a multi-published author with The Wild Rose Press and Trifecta Publishing, and is self-published. To be alerted to her new releases, you can join Marie's newsletter or check out her website: www.mairetuhart.com

OTHER BOOKS BY MARIE TUHART

Her Desert Prince (Desert Destiny)
Her Desert Doctor (Desert Destiny)
Her Desert Horseman (Desert Destiny)
Her Desert Protector (Desert Destiny)
Highland Dom (McMillan Passion)

Bound & Teased
Claimed by the Sheikh
Billionaire's Cowboy's Conquest
More of You (Club Crave)
Reflections of you (Club Crave)
Bound to Love You (Club Crave)
Hot for You (Club Crave)
Tempt (Wicked Sanctuary Series)
Entice (Wicked Sanctuary Series)
Seduce (Wicked Sanctuary Series)
Ravish (Wicked Sanctuary Series)
Possess (Wicked Sanctuary Series) Winter 2021
Spring 2022 – Tantalize (Wicked Sanctuary Series)

PREVIEW OF POSSESS

Prologue

"You have to come with me!" Dani begged Allyson.

Allyson Young regarded her friend. "Why?" Allyson turned away so her friend wouldn't see her grin.

"Please."

Allyson stifled her laughter. Only Dani could make one word sound like ten. "A new bookstore, you say?" Allyson worked for the city planner's office, and she hadn't heard anything about a new bookstore.

"Well, sort of."

Allyson turned to face her friend. "Explain, please."

"It's the expansion to Kleinman's."

"The adult store?" Allyson vaguely remembered something about it. Rudy her co-worker, had made some snide remark about being assigned to it instead of her. Especially since the construction was being done by Riggs Construction.

"Yes. They had a small book area and have monthly book club meetings, but since the meetings exploded, Damon decided to expand the shop."

"What do they have book club meetings about?" Allyson was curious.

"Mainly romance books. The spicy, sexy ones."

Allyson laughed. Dani loved those books, Allyson had read a few herself and liked them. "I see. Do I need to change?" She indicated her jeans and black knit shirt with puffy sleeves.

"It's perfect." Dani gave her a hug.

"Thank you for coming with me," Dani said once they

were in Dani's small compact car driving toward the store.

"Sure. I don't understand why you needed me to come with you." Dani went silent, and Allyson glanced over at her. Dani's features were tight, her lips pressed together, and her fingers clenched the steering wheel. "What's going on?"

Dani stopped at a red light and looked at Allyson. "Remember when I told you I dated a guy in college?"

"Yeah, but you never told me who it was." Dani had gone to the University of Washington for horticulture and landscaping. Allyson had stayed and gone to a community college in Pleasant Valley to learn about the planner's office. "You left right after you graduated to intern with a company in San Francisco."

"Right, and I came back when Gramps got sick last year." The light turned green. "Well, my college ex is going to be there."

"Oh? Do I know him?"

"You might. He works for Riggs Construction."

"It's not the owner, is it?" Allyson liked Zeke. His brown eyes would dance when he smiled and all those muscles… She wanted to run her hands over them. She and Zeke had been dancing around each other for months. Her body went from zero to hot and bothered in about six seconds. Allyson could fall fast for Zeke, but she wasn't sure if she was ready to leap head first into a new relationship since her last one had crashed and burned, the latest in a string of failed relationships. "Wait a second. You've been back for almost a year, and you haven't seen him?"

"No." Dani's cheeks turned red. "I've been avoiding him."

"Why?" That wasn't like her friend.

"It's complicated." Dani pulled into the almost full parking lot. "Wow, looks like there's a lot of people here."

"It's their grand opening?"

"Kind of." Dani found a spot and parked.

"What do you mean?" Her friend was holding something back.

"It was by invitation only."

"So I'm crashing?"

"No." Dani answered. "I'm allowed to bring someone one. You're my plus one."

Allyson blew out a breath. "Okay. Why didn't you just RSVP in the negative?"

"Because I was expected to attend." Dani waved her hands in the air. "Again, it's complicated." Dani blew out a breath. "Look, if you'd rather not come inside, I get it."

"No, it's not that." It wasn't. She'd support Dani in any way she needed. "I'm just wondering why you're being so secretive about it?"

"I don't mean to be, but I did some landscaping work for Damon at his home. So he invited me, and I feel obligated to go."

"And your ex-college lover is going to be here?"

"Yep." Dani dropped her forehead to the steering wheel. "This was a bad idea."

"It's okay." Allyson put her hand on Dani's shoulder. "We go in, we mingle, and after an hour, we leave."

"Thank you." They got out of the car.

Allyson wasn't sure what she expected, but the storefront was tastefully decorated with balloons and steamers. She walked in behind Dani.

"Dani, glad you could make it." A dark-haired man hugged Dani with a smile.

"Hey, Damon. I didn't want to miss it. This is my

friend, Allyson.”

"Well, hello there." He took her hand and kissed the back of it. "Aren't you a delicious morsel."

Allyson frowned.

"Damon, behave." A woman with light brown hair joined them. Her voice held laughter as she slapped him on the arm. "Excuse him. He's a flirt. Hi, I'm Tessa." She held out her hand.

Damon let out a sigh and released Allyson's hand.

"Allyson, Dani's friend."

"Well, any friend of Dani's is one of ours. Please feel free to look around. There is finger food and drinks are over there." Tessa pointed to where a group of people milled around.

"Thanks, Tessa." Dani took her by the arm and led her away from the couple.

"So he owns the place?" Allyson asked.

"Yes. Tessa's his girlfriend. I don't think they've gotten engaged yet."

"So why was he flirting with me?" She frowned. That wasn't very nice of Damon.

"That's just Damon. Trust me, he wouldn't do a thing to hurt Tessa."

"Hummm."

"Allyson."

She turned at the sound of her name.

"Hi, Zeke." What was he doing there? He looked delicious in those jeans and a tight black T-shirt.

"Hey, Zeke," Dani said.

"Dani." His gaze went from Dani to Allyson. "You two friends?"

"Yes." Dani said. "Oh I see Lara. I wanted to chat with her." Dani left, and Allyson looked up at Zeke.

"I understand you did the remodel?" she asked, trying to stay calm. Dani just walked away without a second thought.

"Yep. I did." He grinned. "I'm sorry you weren't assigned the job. Your co-worker can be a pain."

Allyson grimaced. "I want to say I'm sorry, but I really don't have control over him." Why Rudy made such snide remarks about this place she didn't know. It looked like typical bookstore to her.

"I know. Shall we?" He held out his arm.

Manners. She'd almost forgotten men had them. "Thank you." She slipped her arm through his. It was nice to be treated like a woman instead of another guy. Yes, she worked with a lot of men, and they did forget she was female.

"Do you want something to eat or drink? Or would you rather have a tour of the bookstore?"

"Are you playing guide?" She fluttered her lashes at him, wondering where this vixen inside her had come from. Hadn't she just convinced herself this wouldn't go well?

Zeke laughed. "I'm offering my services, yes." He leaned down. "More than just a tour guide, if you're interested."

Allyson started to pull back to berate him, but stopped herself. She wanted to know more about Zeke. "Let's see how today goes, and we'll go from there."

"I can agree to that. At least you're not running."

"When did I run?" Had she done that to him?

"That wasn't the right word. Usually, you brush off my attempts to get to know you better."

"Sorry." She lowered her gaze. "I'd just come off a pretty bad break up." The jackass ex had thought he could order her around in the bedroom and out of it. He got a rude awakening.

"I'm sorry."

"Don't be. He was an ass." She glanced at the first bookshelf. Oh my. Alternative lifestyles. Her heart pounded.

"Well then, he didn't deserve you." He rubbed his thumb over the back of her hand. "Damon's bookstore is as tasteful as the adult store is."

"Oh, I've never been inside an adult store." In a way, that was funny. She'd dabbled in kink but had never gone into an adult store.

"I'd love to educate you, if you're willing."

"I might take you up on that, Mr. Riggs."

www.ingramcontent.com/pod-product-compliance
Lightning Source LLC
Chambersburg PA
CBHW070930190726
48292CB00004B/1188